a blue apple for you!

Copyright © 2009 by Lark Pien
All rights reserved / CIP Data is available.
Published in the United States 2009 by
🍎 Blue Apple Books
515 Valley Street, Maplewood, NJ 07040
www.blueapplebooks.com

02/15
Printed in Korea
ISBN: 978-1-934706-44-2

3 5 7 9 10 8 6 4 2

Long Tail Kitty

by Lark Pien

🍎 Blue Apple Books

To the old artnight crew

Thanks

Jesse Reklaw for the design and engineering of LTK's font

Kip and Sam for their long standing LTK friendship

Jane Pien for the LTK finger puppets

Thien Pham for the LTKE (long tail kitty everything)

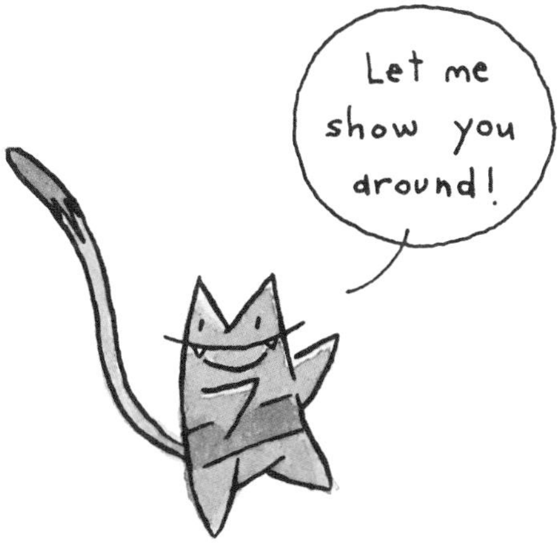
Let me show you around!

Where I Live

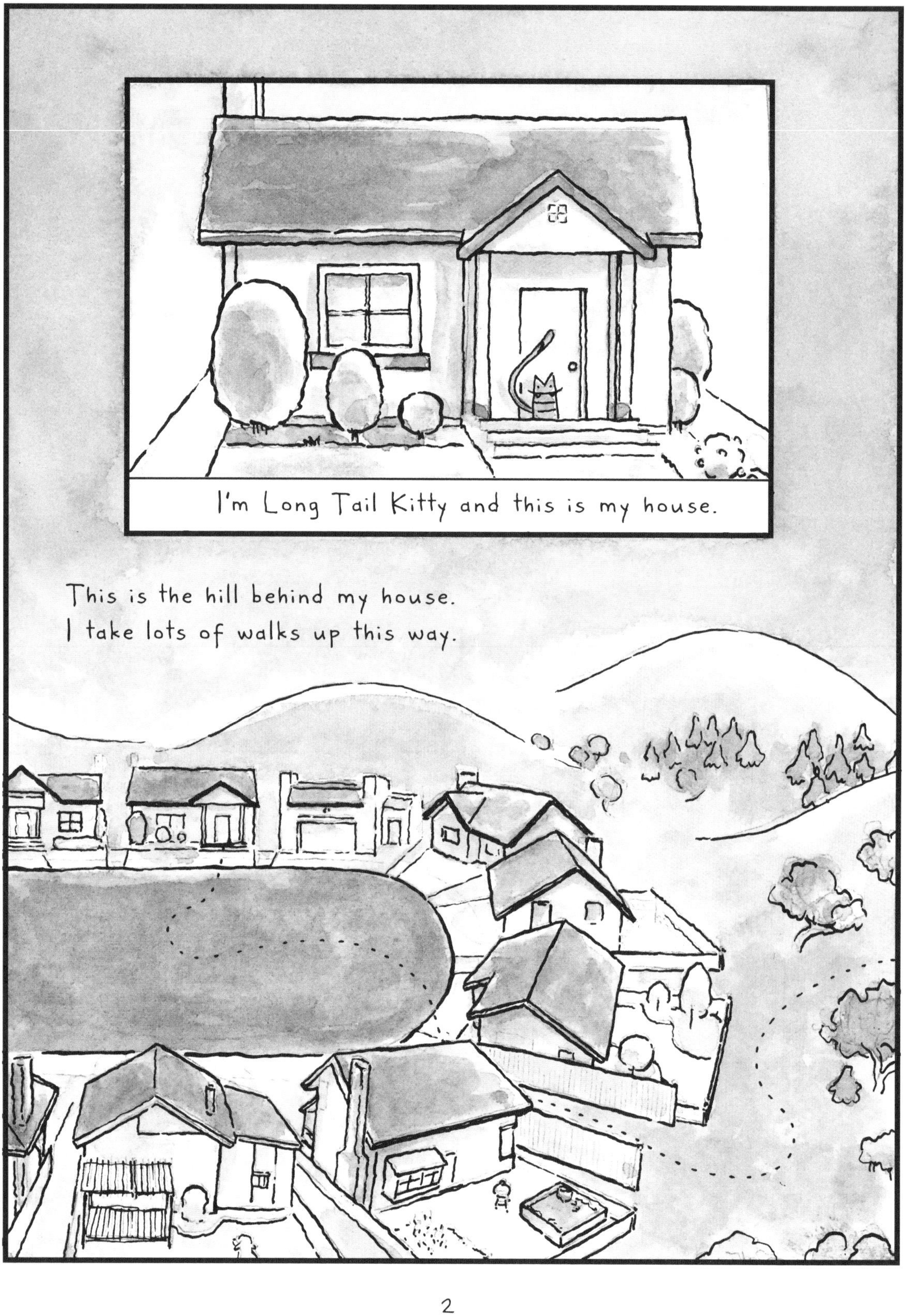
I'm Long Tail Kitty and this is my house.
This is the hill behind my house.
I take lots of walks up this way.

On the other side of the hill there is a meadow; many flowers bloom. It is also where I got stung by a bee!

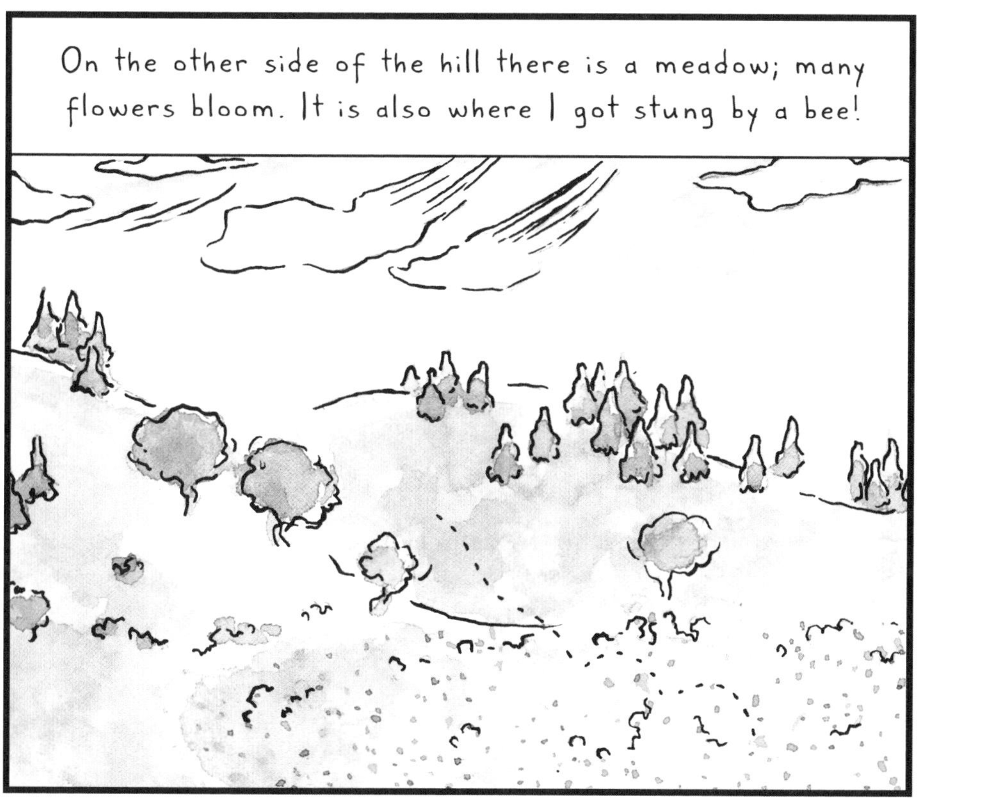

By the meadow there is a lake. In the winter, the lake freezes and becomes ice.

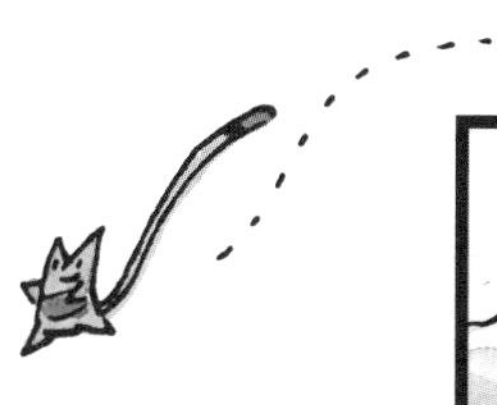

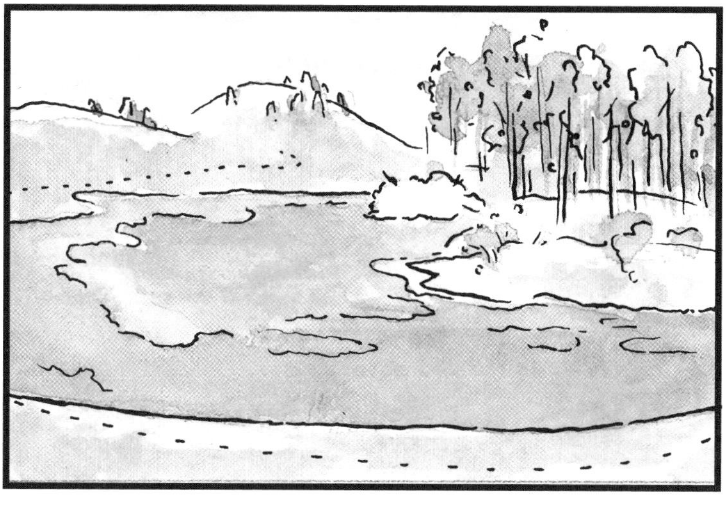

It is where my friend Good Tall Mouse likes to skate.

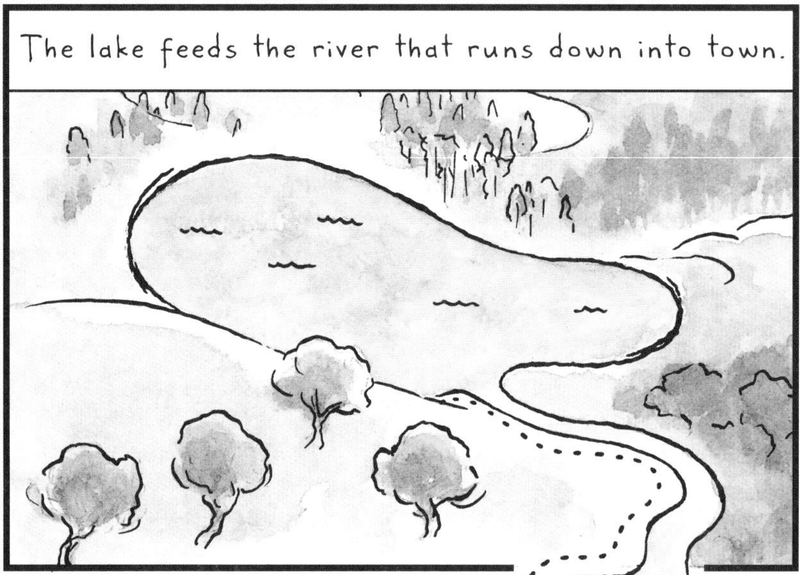
The lake feeds the river that runs down into town.

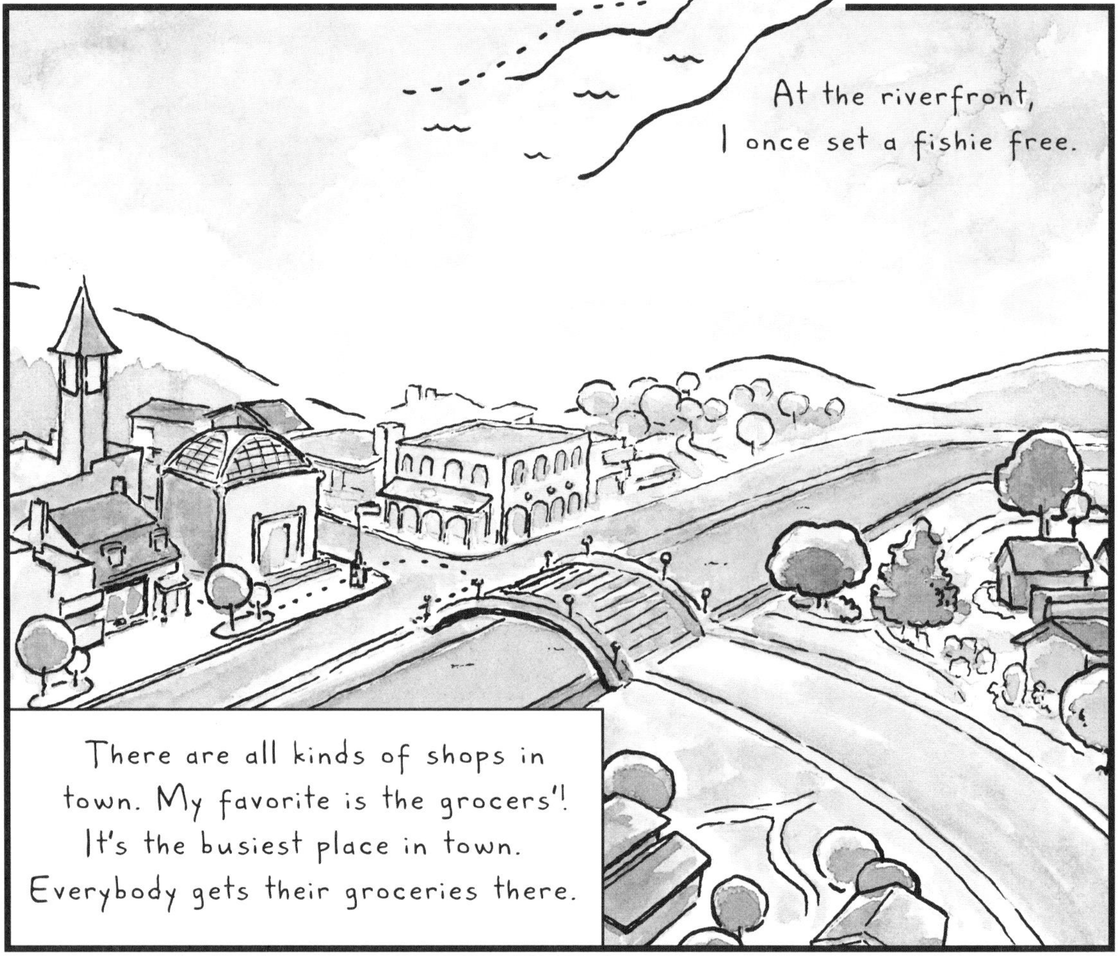
At the riverfront,
I once set a fishie free.
There are all kinds of shops in town. My favorite is the grocers'!
It's the busiest place in town.
Everybody gets their groceries there.

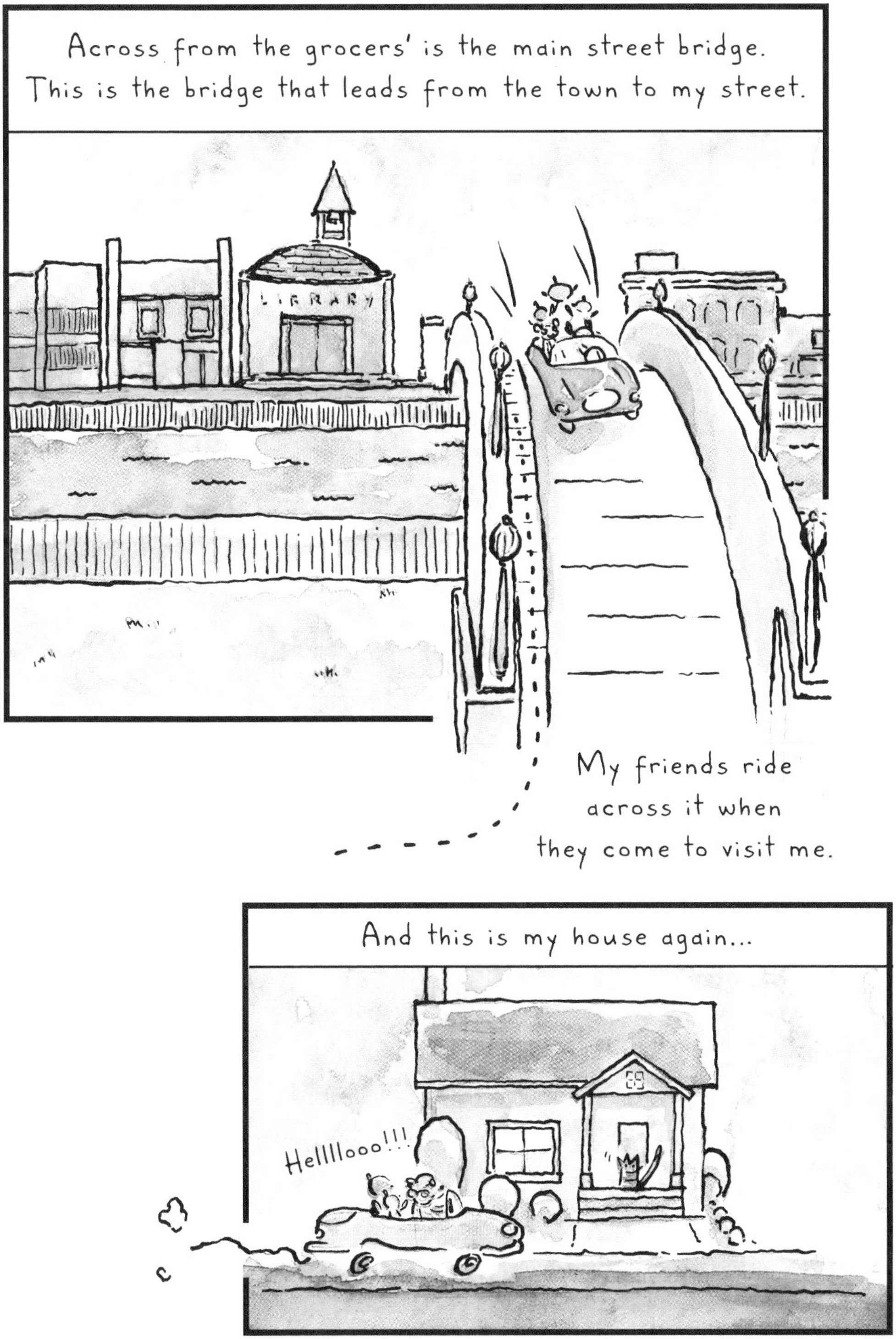
Across from the grocers' is the main street bridge.
This is the bridge that leads from the town to my street.
LIBRARY
My friends ride across it when they come to visit me.
And this is my house again...
Hellllooo!!!

by the hill, by the meadow,
by the lake, by the river,
by the town, by the bridge,
on the street where I live.

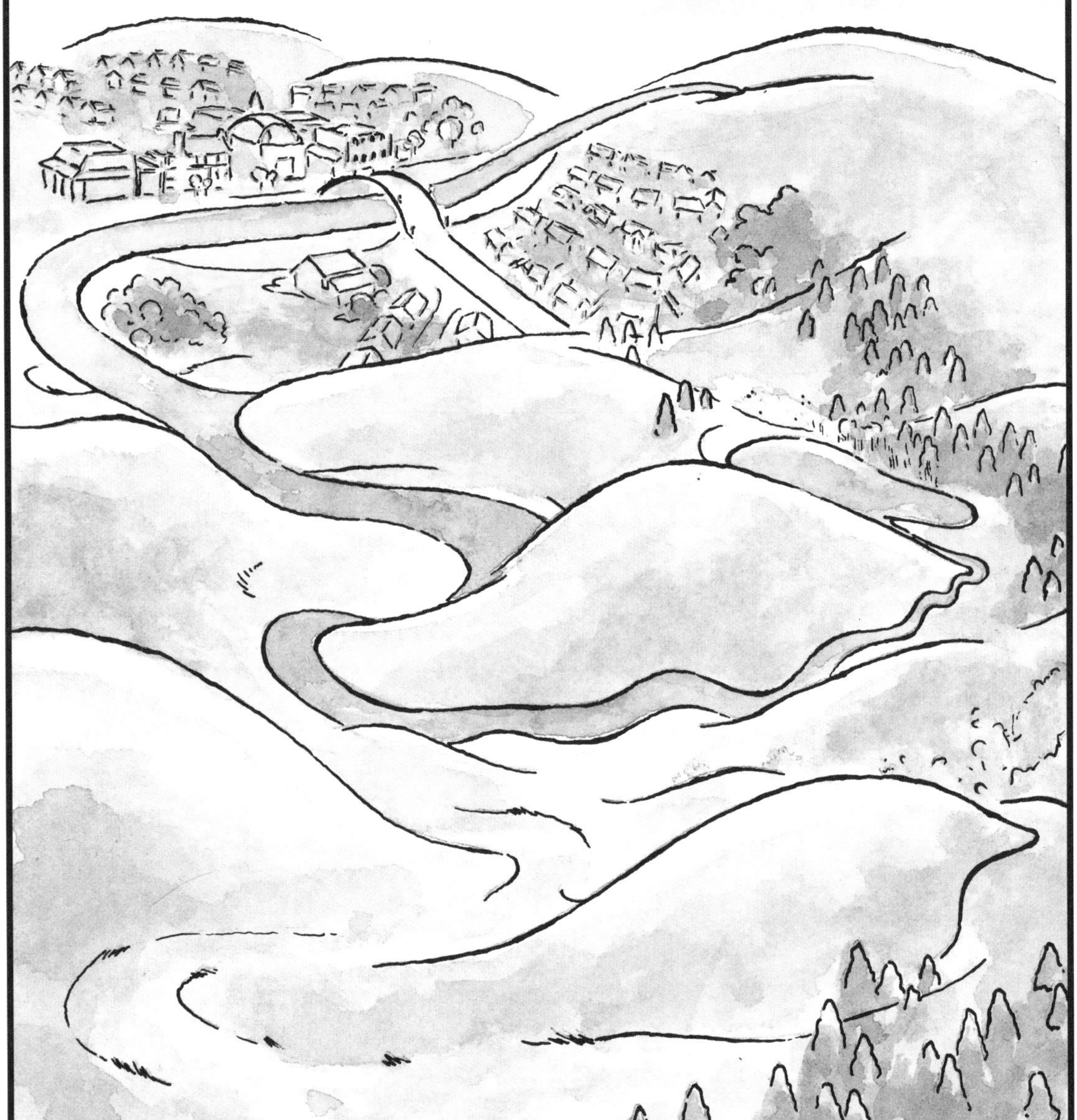

What a Sting
Can Bring

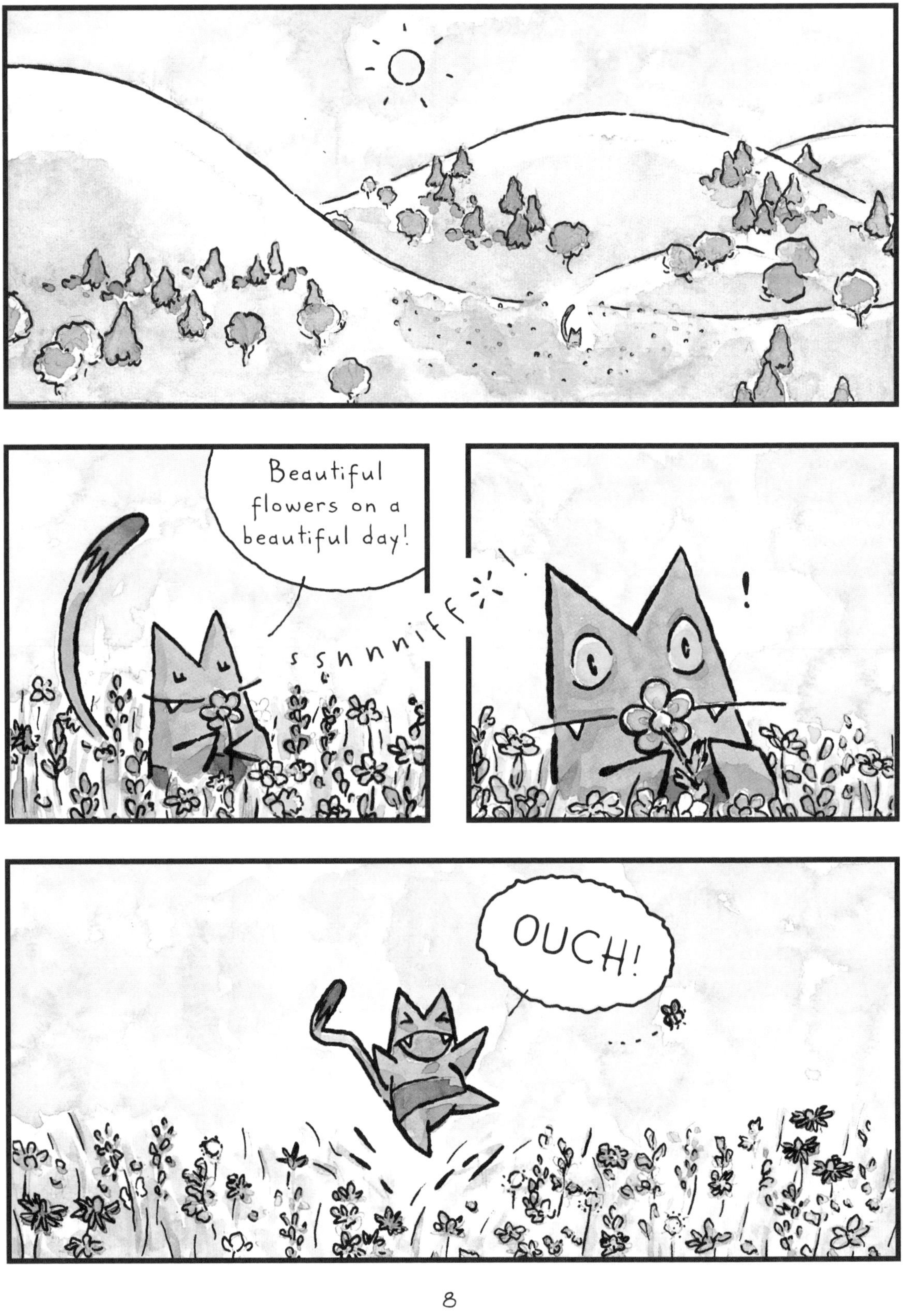

Beautiful flowers on a beautiful day!
ssnnniff
!
OUCH!

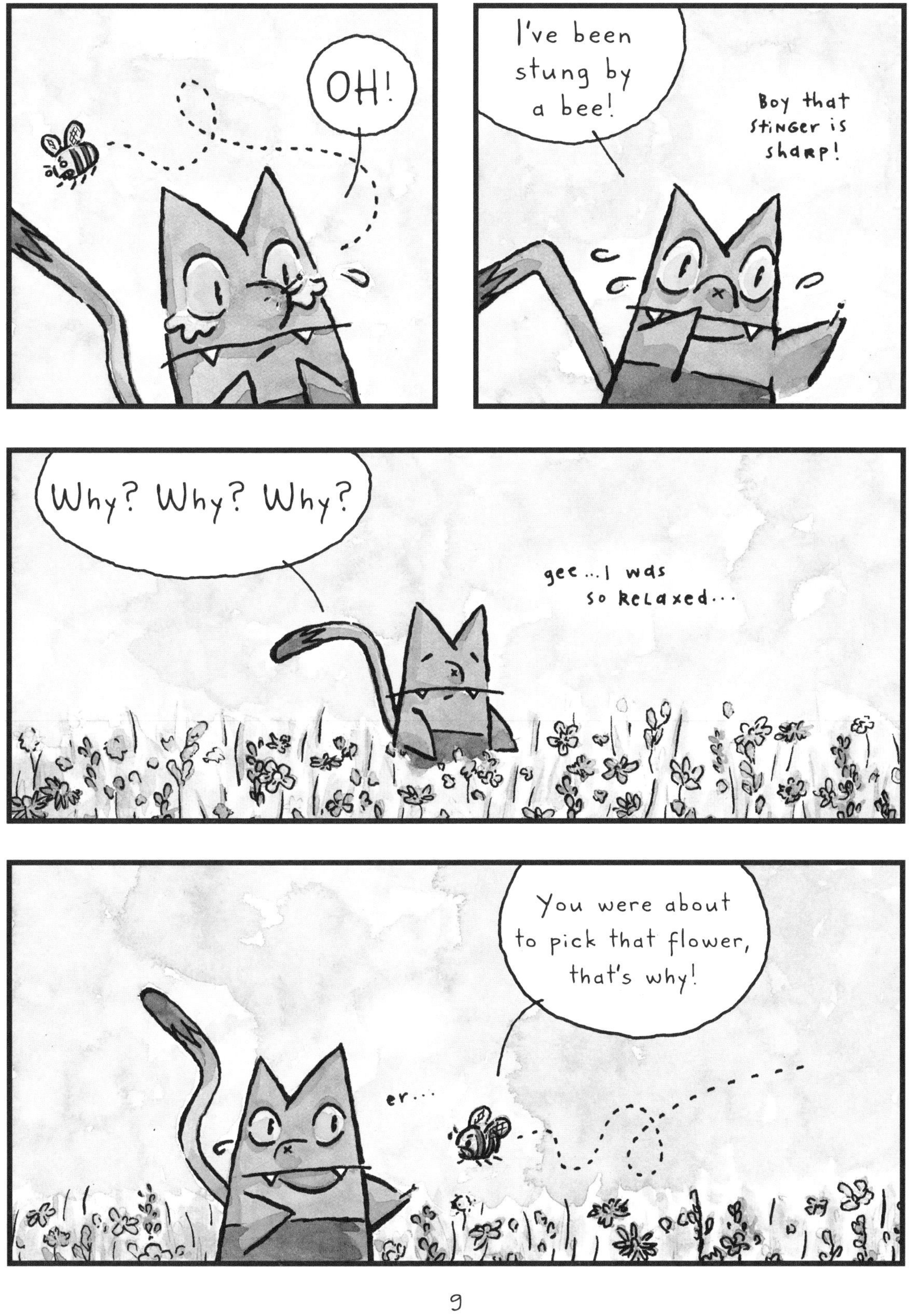
OH!
I've been stung by a bee!
Boy that stinger is sharp!
Why? Why? Why?
gee...I was so relaxed...
You were about to pick that flower, that's why!
er...

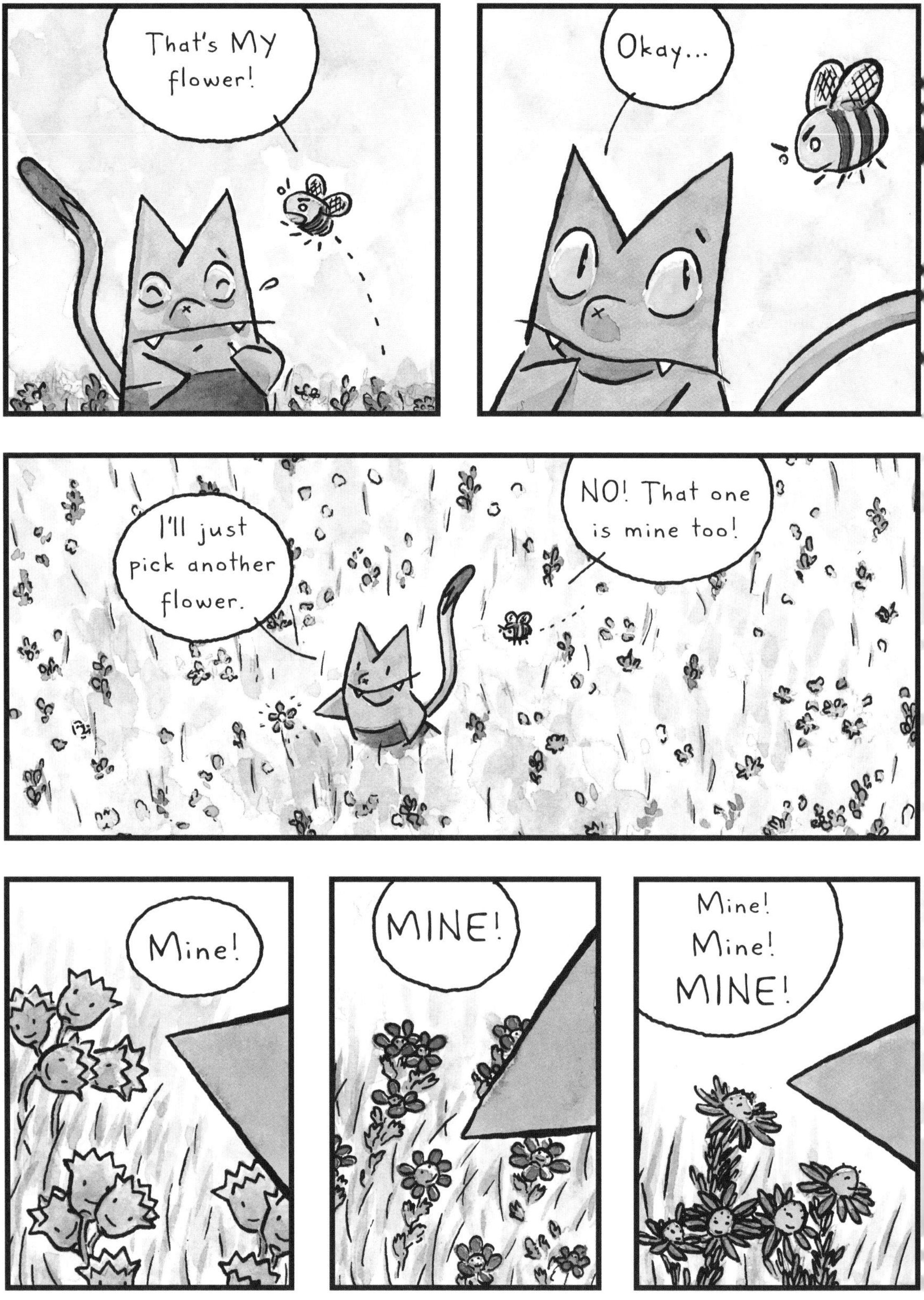
That's MY flower!
Okay...
I'll just pick another flower.
NO! That one is mine too!
Mine!
MINE!
Mine! Mine! MINE!

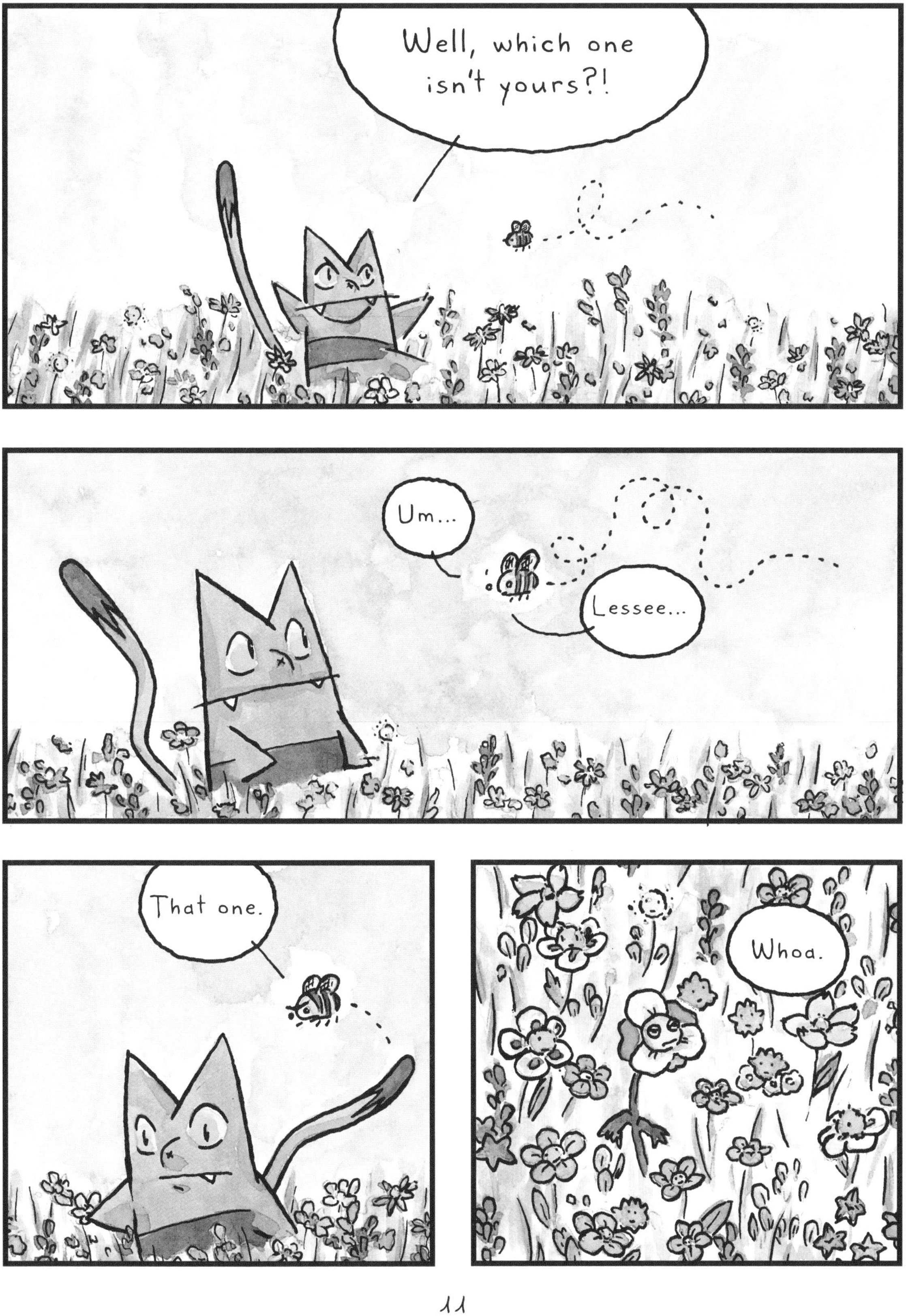
Well, which one isn't yours?!
Um...
Lessee...
That one.
Whoa.

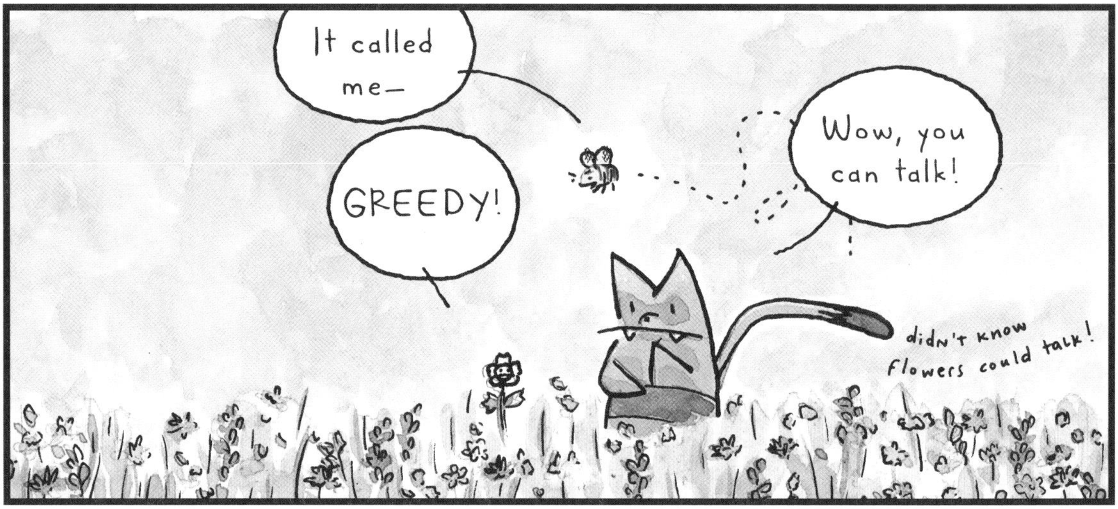
It called me–
GREEDY!
Wow, you can talk!
didn't know flowers could talk!

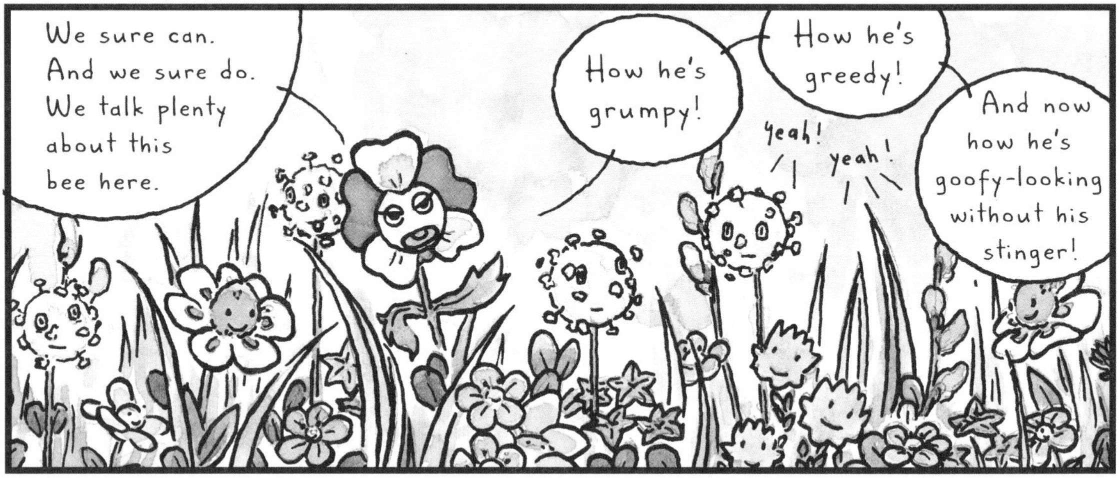
We sure can. And we sure do. We talk plenty about this bee here.
How he's grumpy!
How he's greedy!
yeah!
yeah!
And now how he's goofy-looking without his stinger!

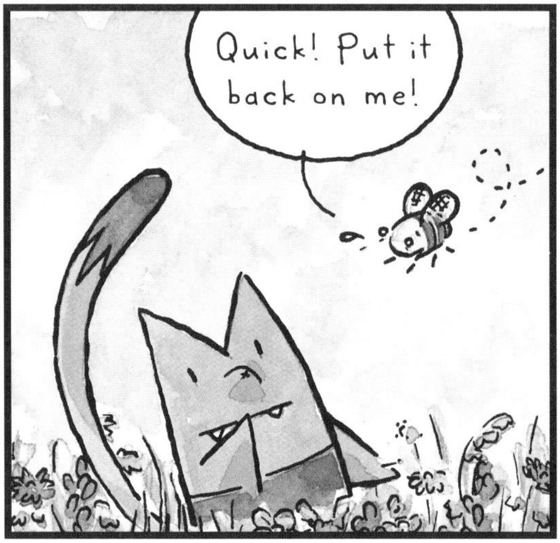
Quick! Put it back on me!

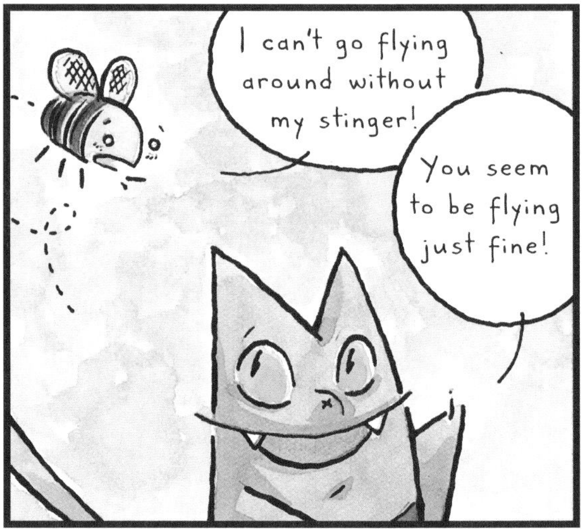
I can't go flying around without my stinger!
You seem to be flying just fine!

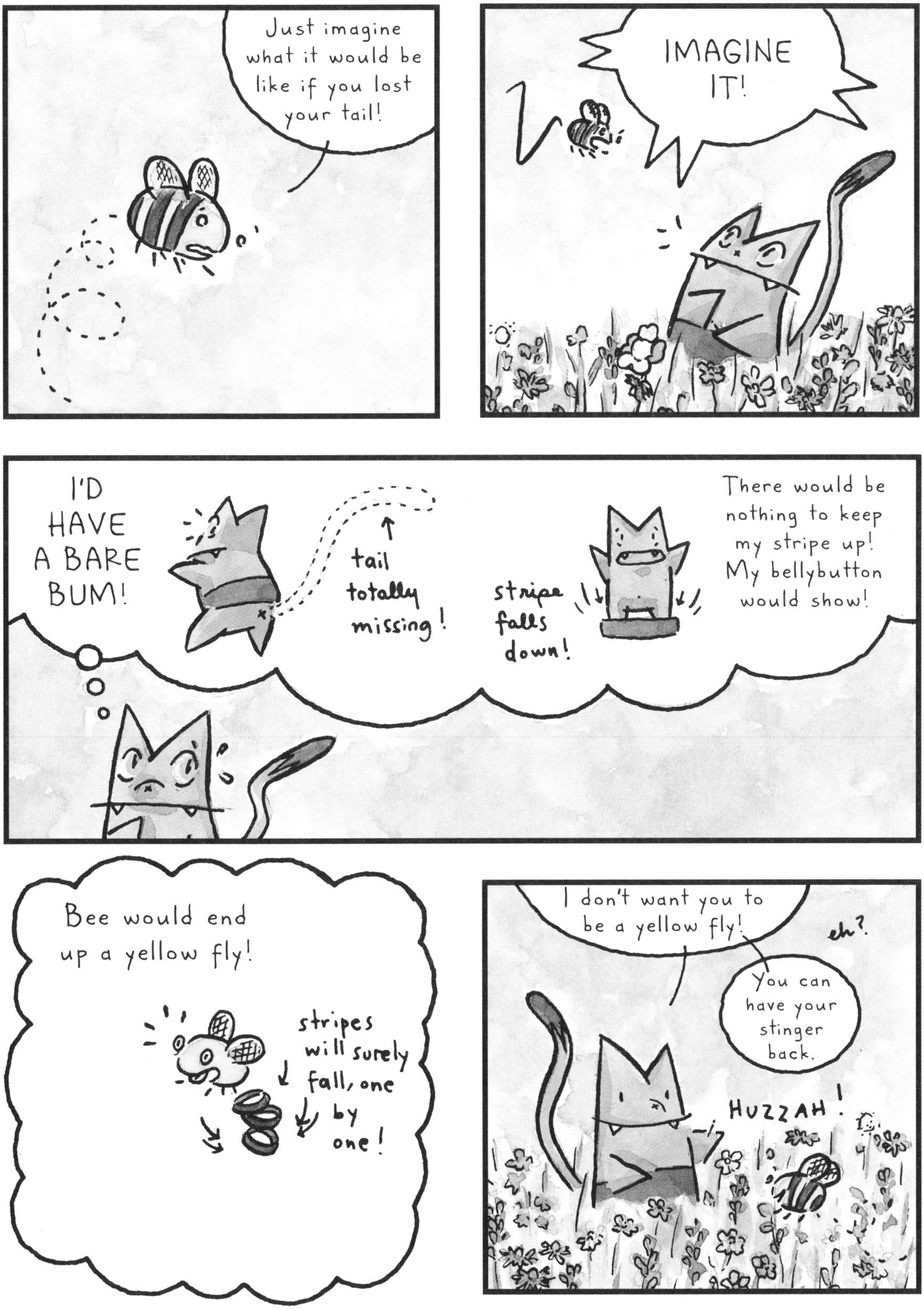
Just imagine what it would be like if you lost your tail!
IMAGINE IT!
I'D HAVE A BARE BUM!
tail totally missing!
stripe falls down!
There would be nothing to keep my stripe up! My bellybutton would show!
Bee would end up a yellow fly!
stripes will surely fall, one by one!
I don't want you to be a yellow fly!
eh?
You can have your stinger back.
HUZZAH!

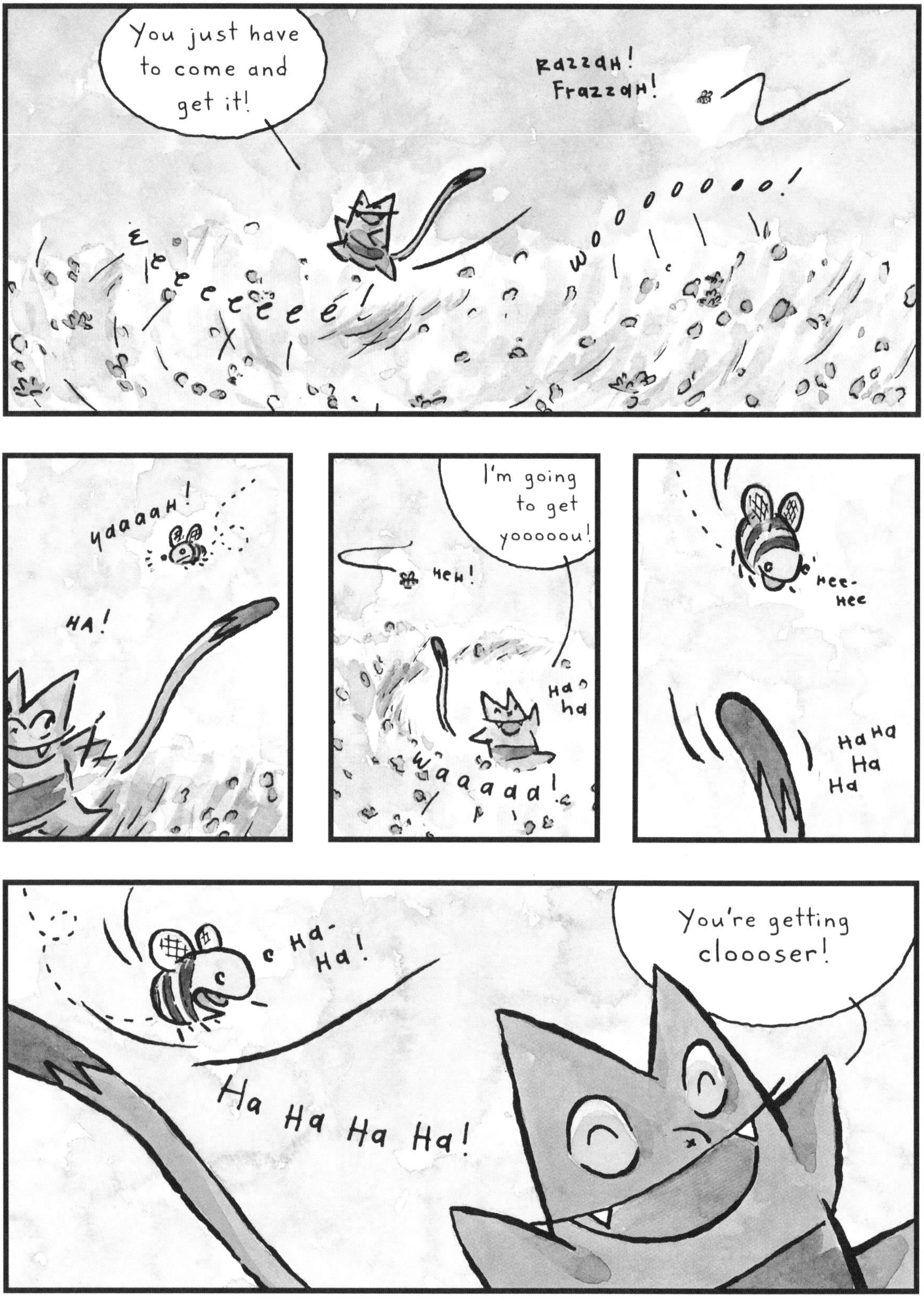
You just have to come and get it!
Razzah! Frazzah!
Eeeeeeeee!
Woooooooo!
yaaaah!
HA!
I'm going to get yoooou!
Heh!
Ha ha
Waaaaaa!
Hee-hee
Ha Ha Ha Ha
Ha-Ha!
Ha Ha Ha Ha!
You're getting cloooser!

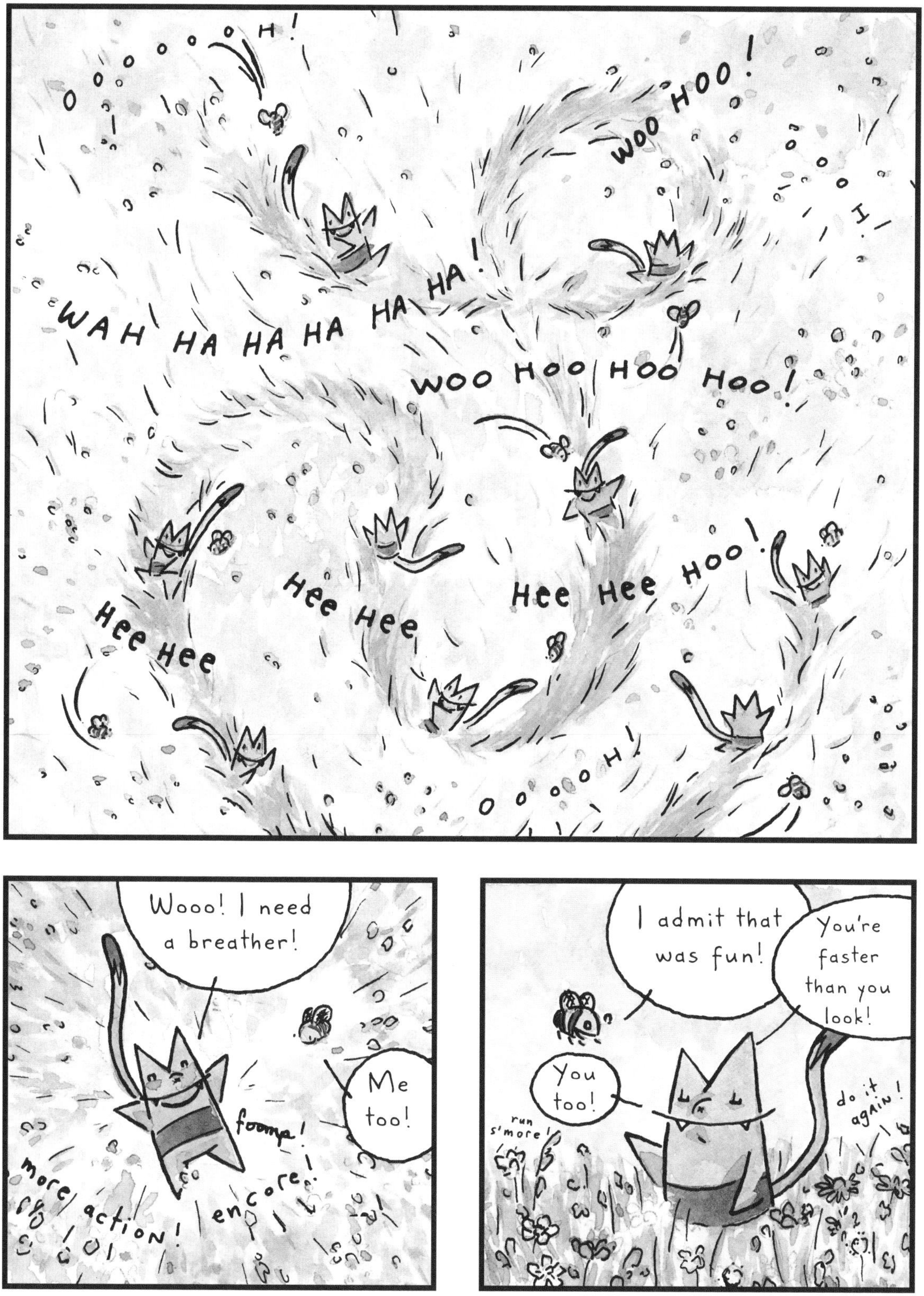
OOOOOOH!
WOO HOO!
OOOOH!
WAH HA HA HA HA HA!
WOO HOO HOO HOO!
Hee Hee
Hee Hee
Hee Hee Hoo!
OOOOOOH!
Wooo! I need a breather!
Me too!
foomp!
more action!
encore!
I admit that was fun!
You're faster than you look!
You too!
run s'more!
do it AGAIN!

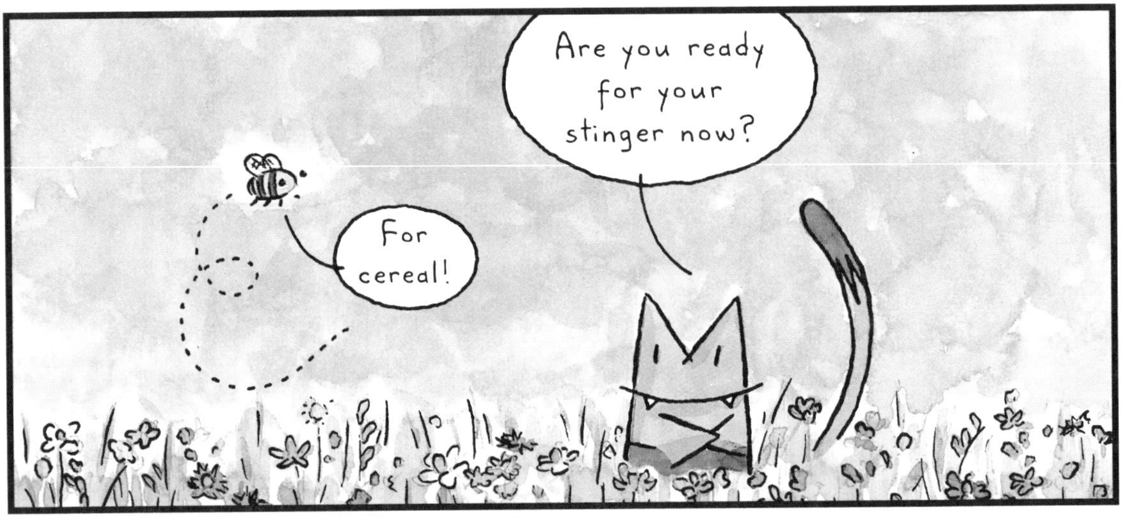
Are you ready for your stinger now?
For cereal!

editor's note: cereal = seriously + for real

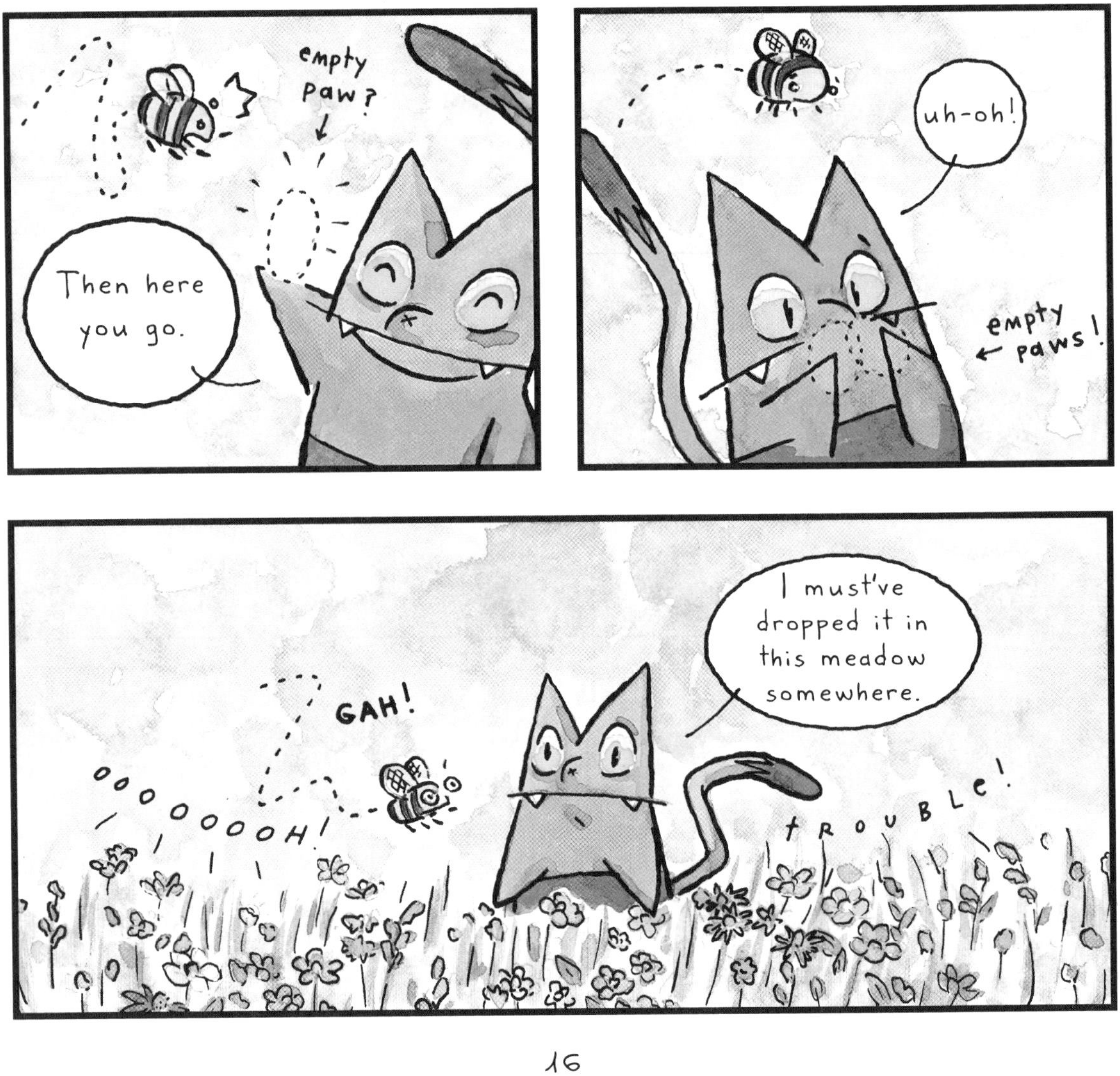
empty paw?
Then here you go.
uh-oh!
empty paws!
I must've dropped it in this meadow somewhere.
GAH!
OOOOOOOOH!
TROUBLE!

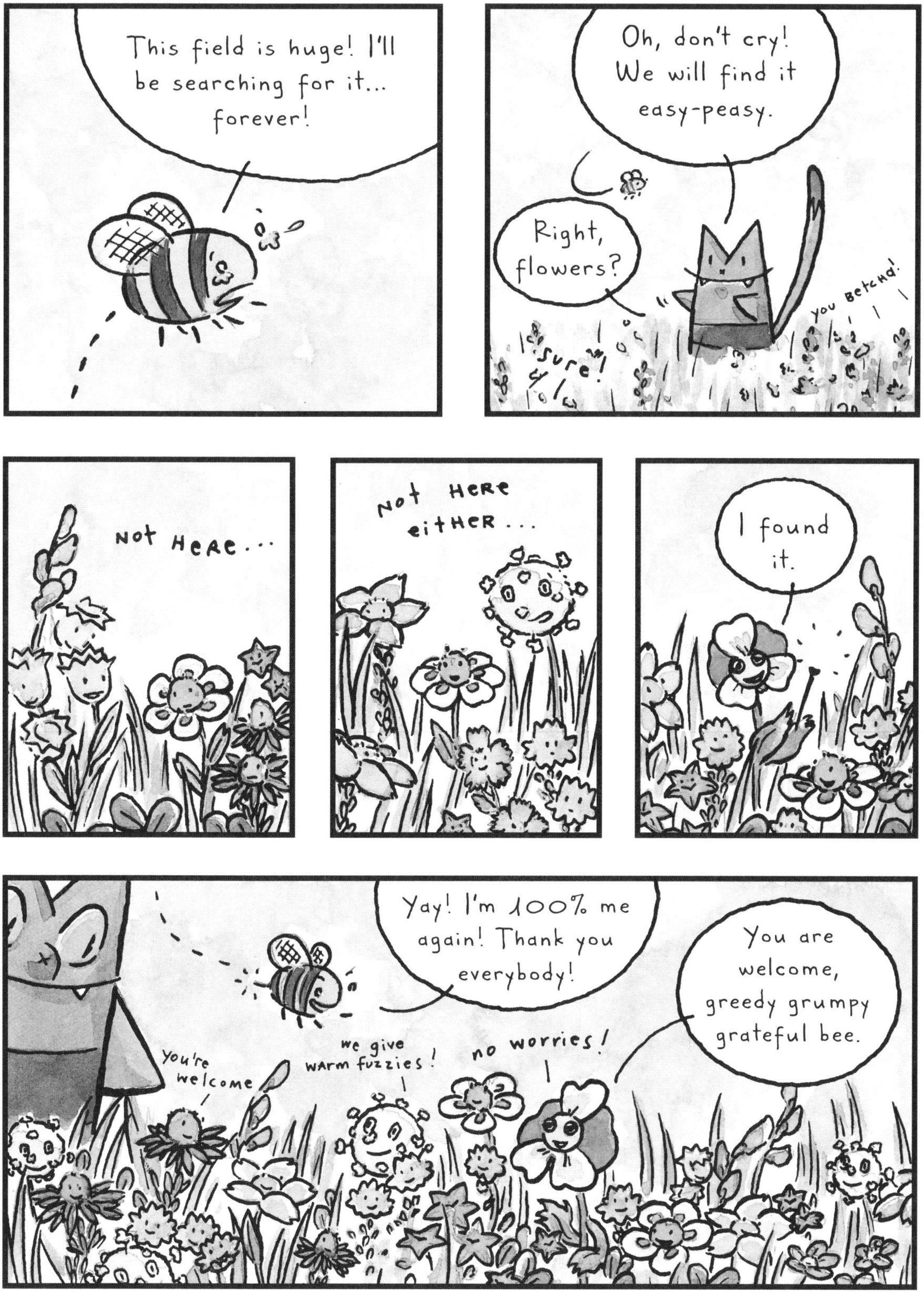
This field is huge! I'll be searching for it... forever!
Oh, don't cry! We will find it easy-peasy.
Right, flowers?
sure!
you betcha!
not HeRe...
not HeRe eitHeR...
I found it.
Yay! I'm 100% me again! Thank you everybody!
You are welcome, greedy grumpy grateful bee.
you're welcome
we give warm fuzzies!
no worries!

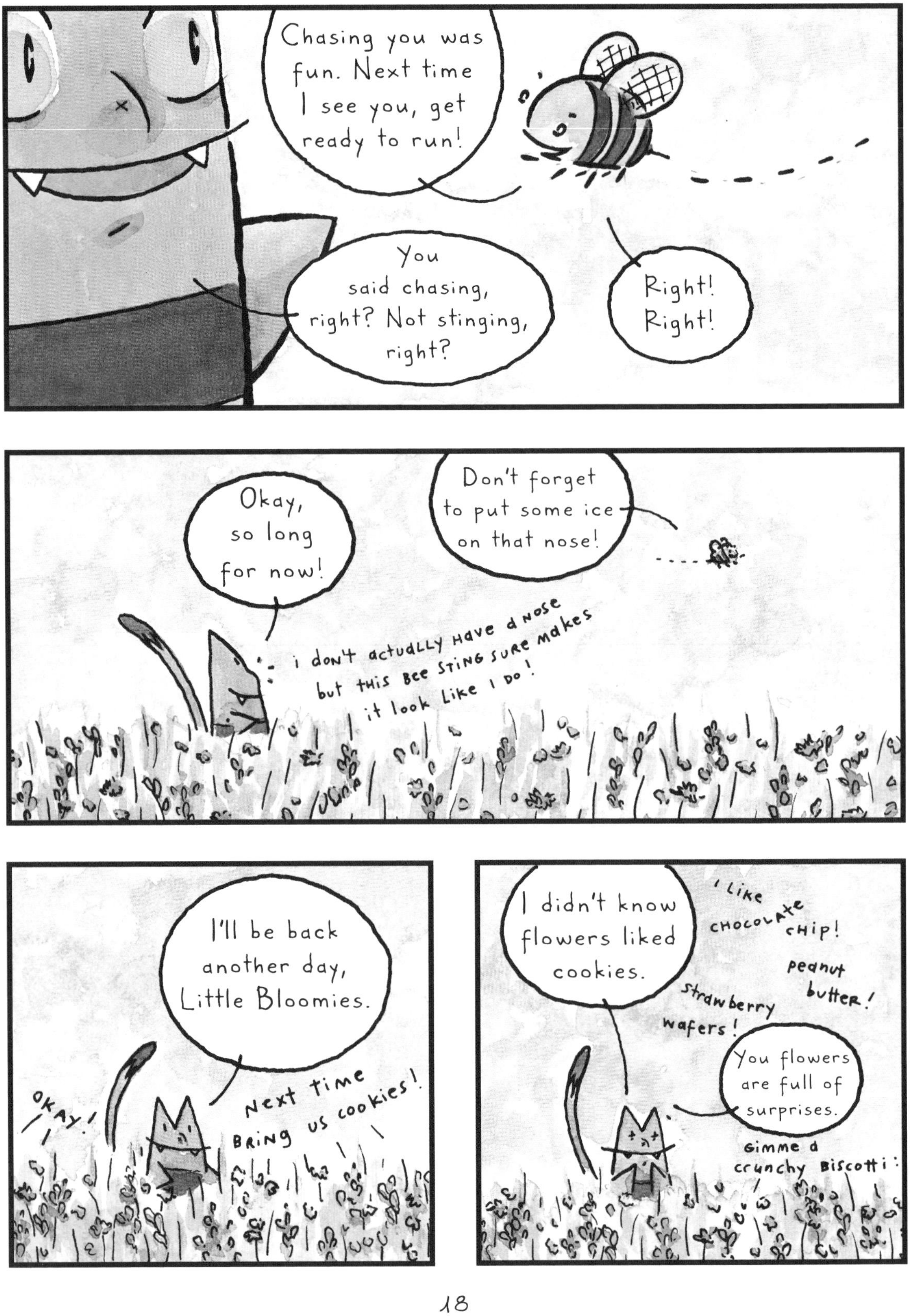
Chasing you was fun. Next time I see you, get ready to run!
You said chasing, right? Not stinging, right?
Right! Right!
Okay, so long for now!
Don't forget to put some ice on that nose!
i don't actually have a nose but this bee sting sure makes it look like i do!
I'll be back another day, Little Bloomies.
Next time bring us cookies!
Okay!
I didn't know flowers liked cookies.
I like chocolate chip!
peanut butter!
strawberry wafers!
You flowers are full of surprises.
Gimme a crunchy biscotti!

You and Me,
What We See

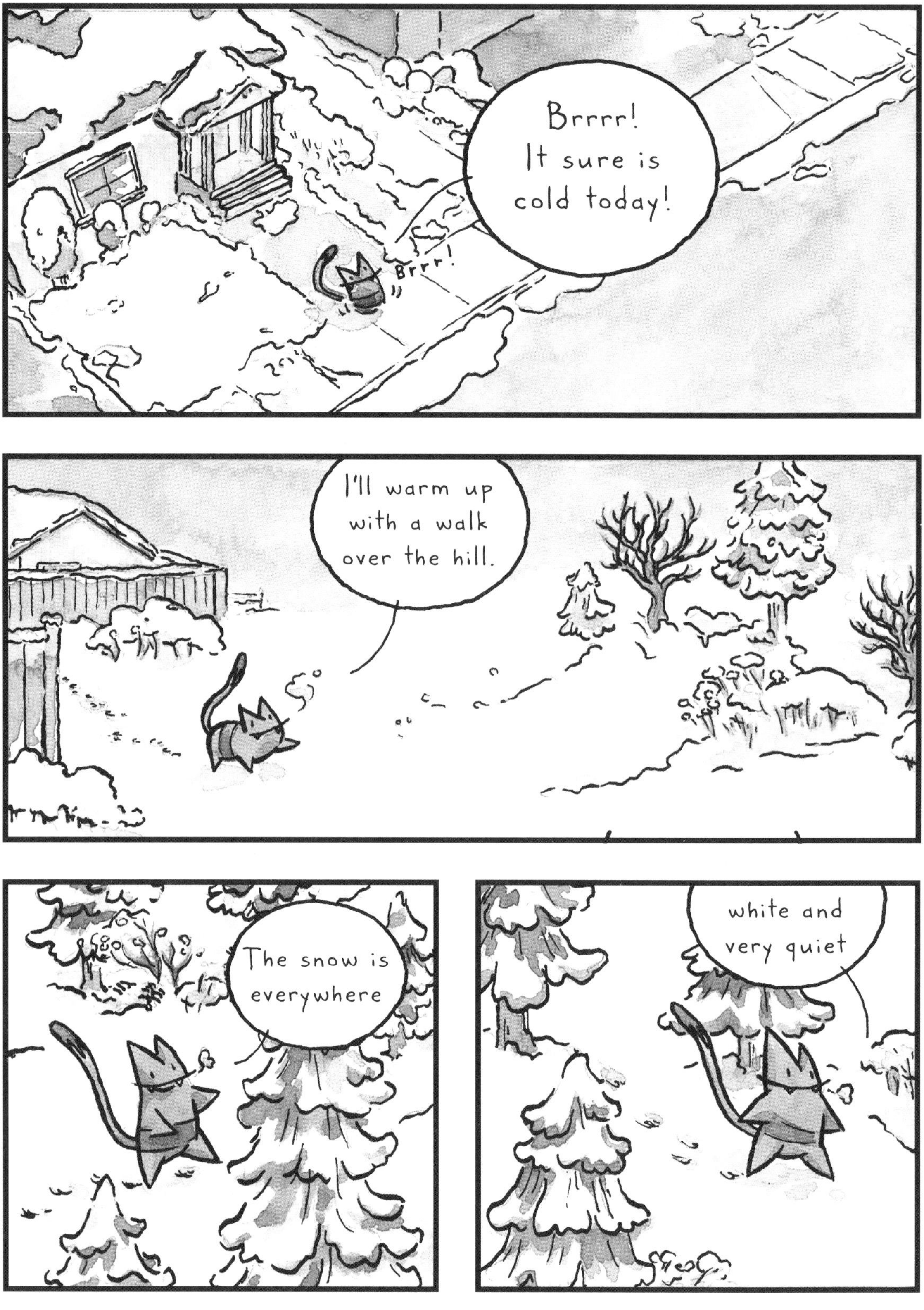
Brrrr!
It sure is
cold today!
Brrr!
I'll warm up
with a walk
over the hill.
The snow is
everywhere
white and
very quiet

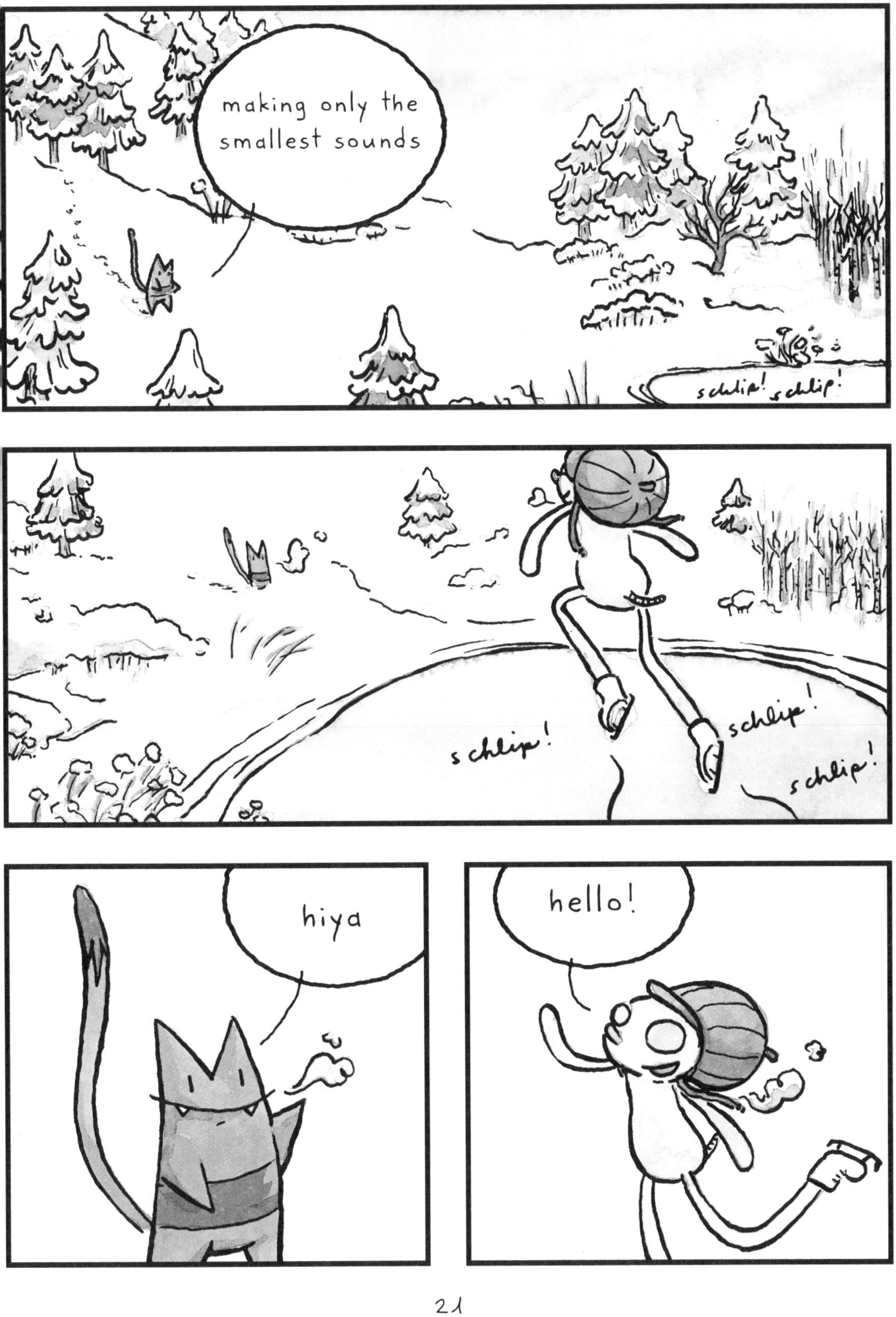
making only the smallest sounds
schlip! schlip!
schlip!
schlip!
schlip!
hiya
hello!

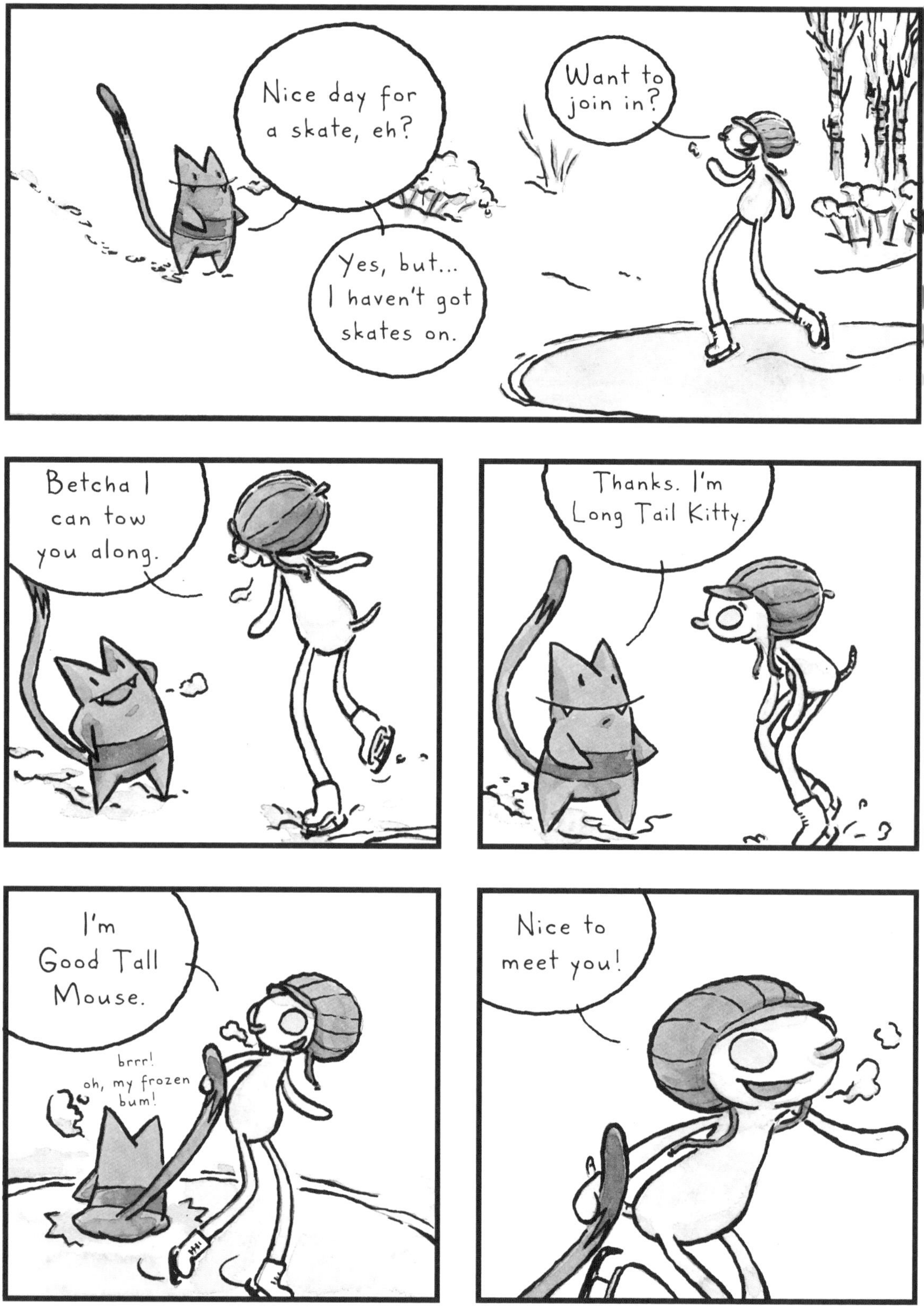
Nice day for a skate, eh?
Yes, but... I haven't got skates on.
Want to join in?
Betcha I can tow you along.
Thanks. I'm Long Tail Kitty.
I'm Good Tall Mouse.
brrr! oh, my frozen bum!
Nice to meet you!

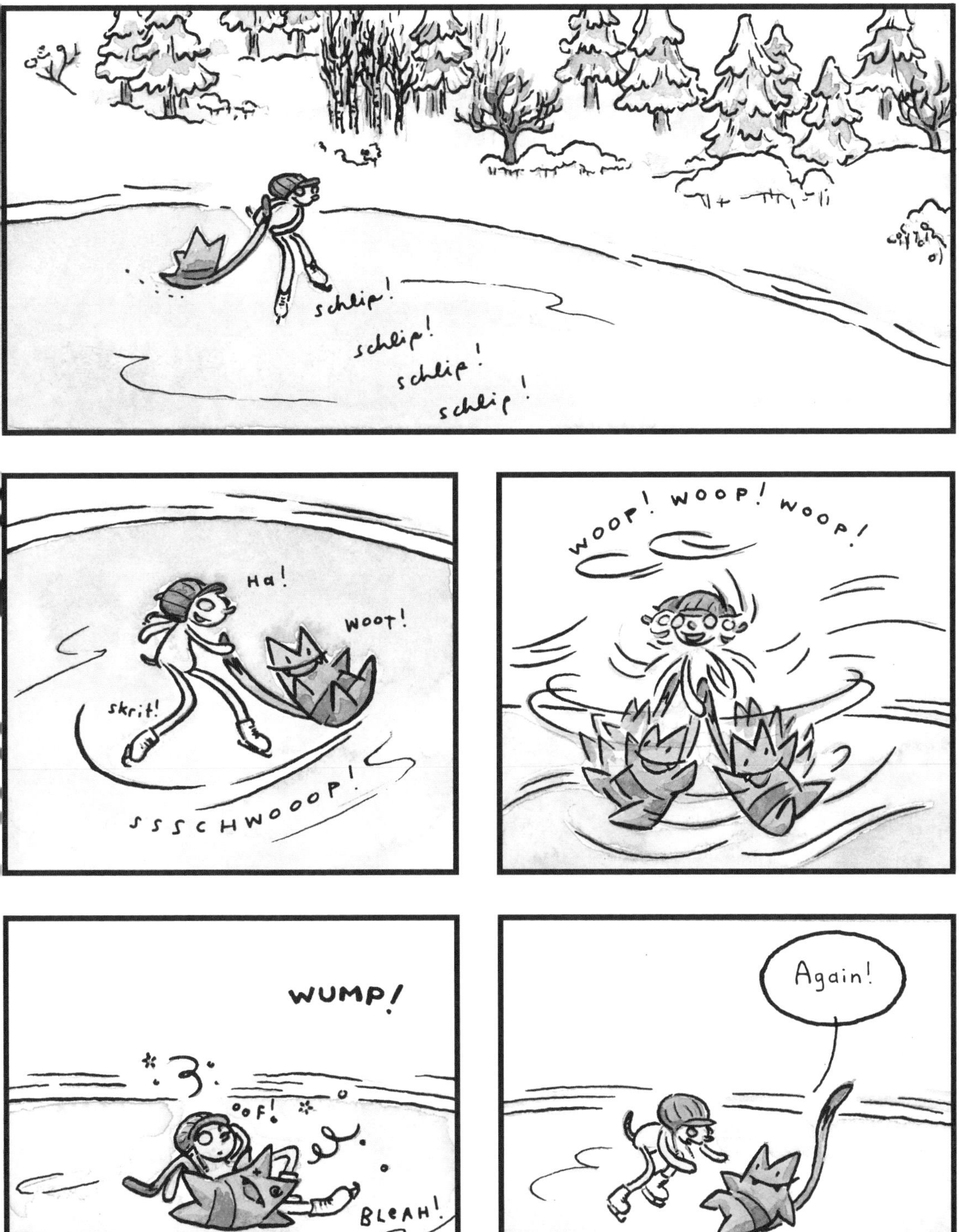
schlip!
schlip!
schlip!
schlip!
Ha!
WOOT!
skrit!
SSSCHWOOOP!
WOOP! WOOP! WOOP!
WUMP!
oof!
BLEAH!
Again!

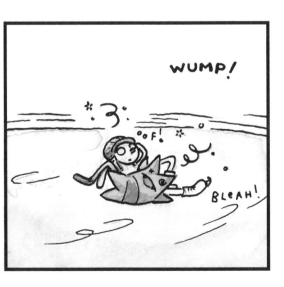

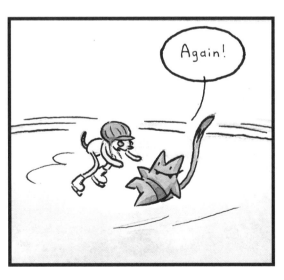

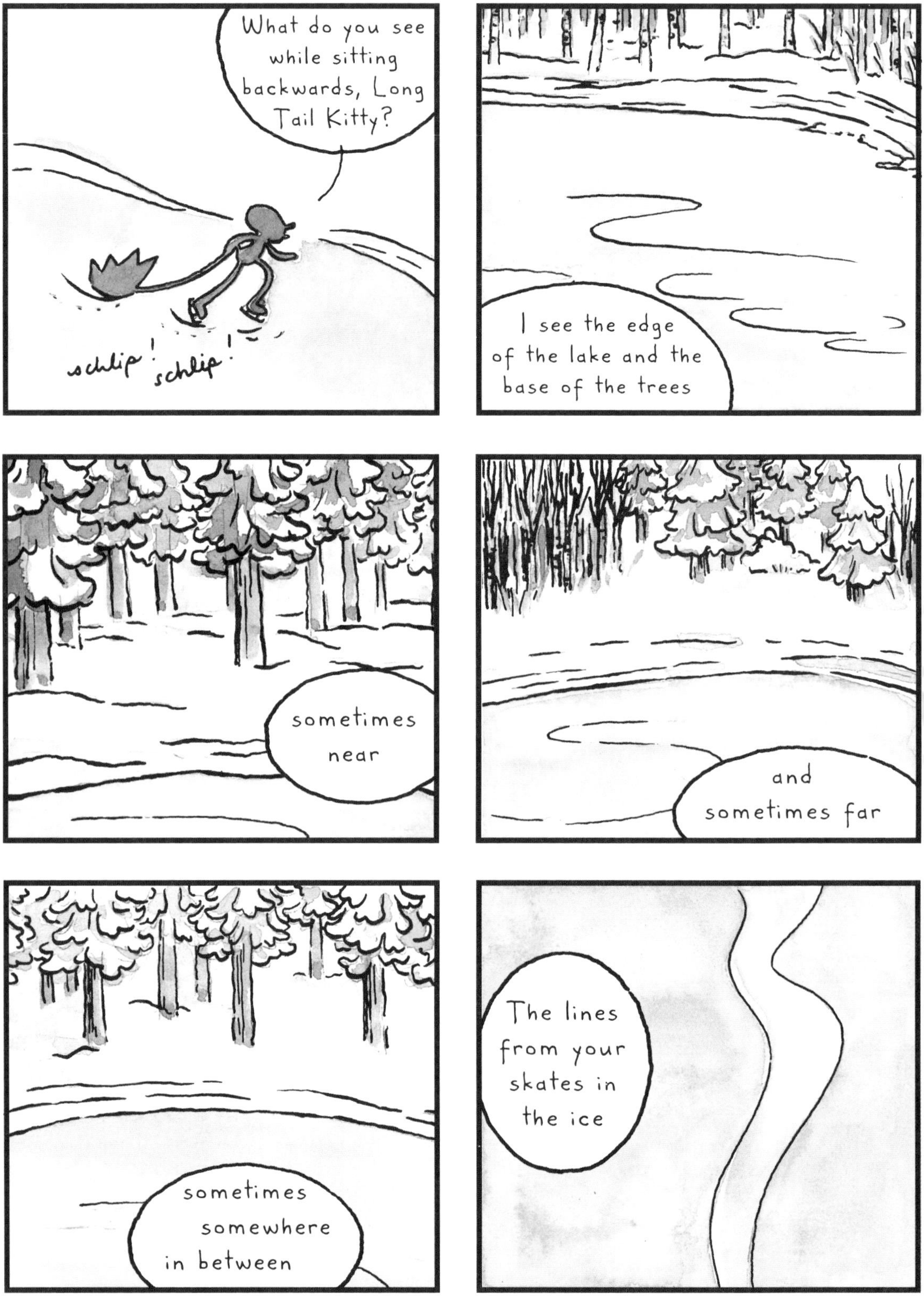
What do you see while sitting backwards, Long Tail Kitty?
schlip! schlip!
I see the edge of the lake and the base of the trees
sometimes near
and sometimes far
sometimes somewhere in between
The lines from your skates in the ice

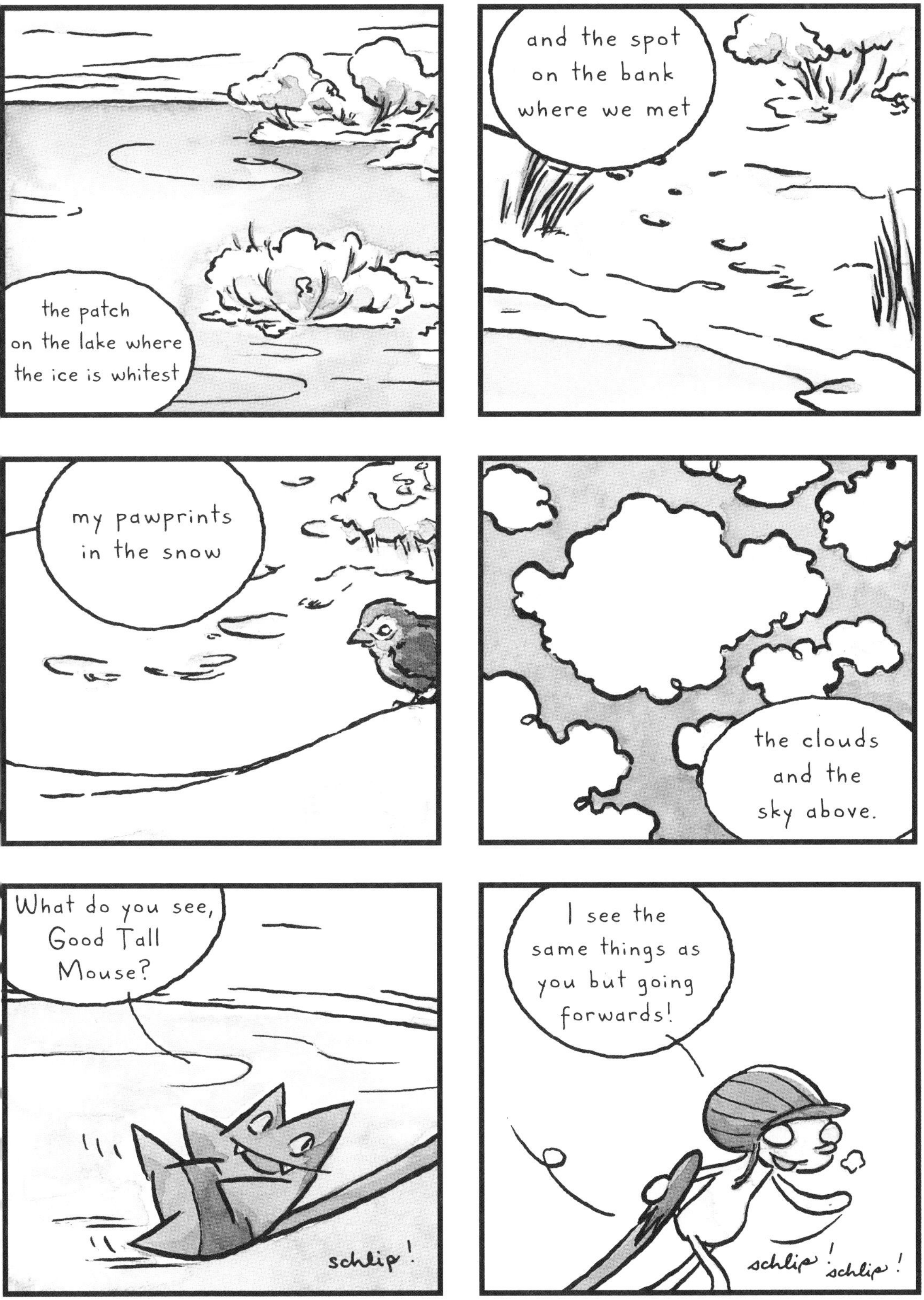
the patch
on the lake where
the ice is whitest
and the spot
on the bank
where we met
my pawprints
in the snow
the clouds
and the
sky above.
What do you see,
Good Tall
Mouse?
schlip!
I see the
same things as
you but going
forwards!
schlip! schlip!

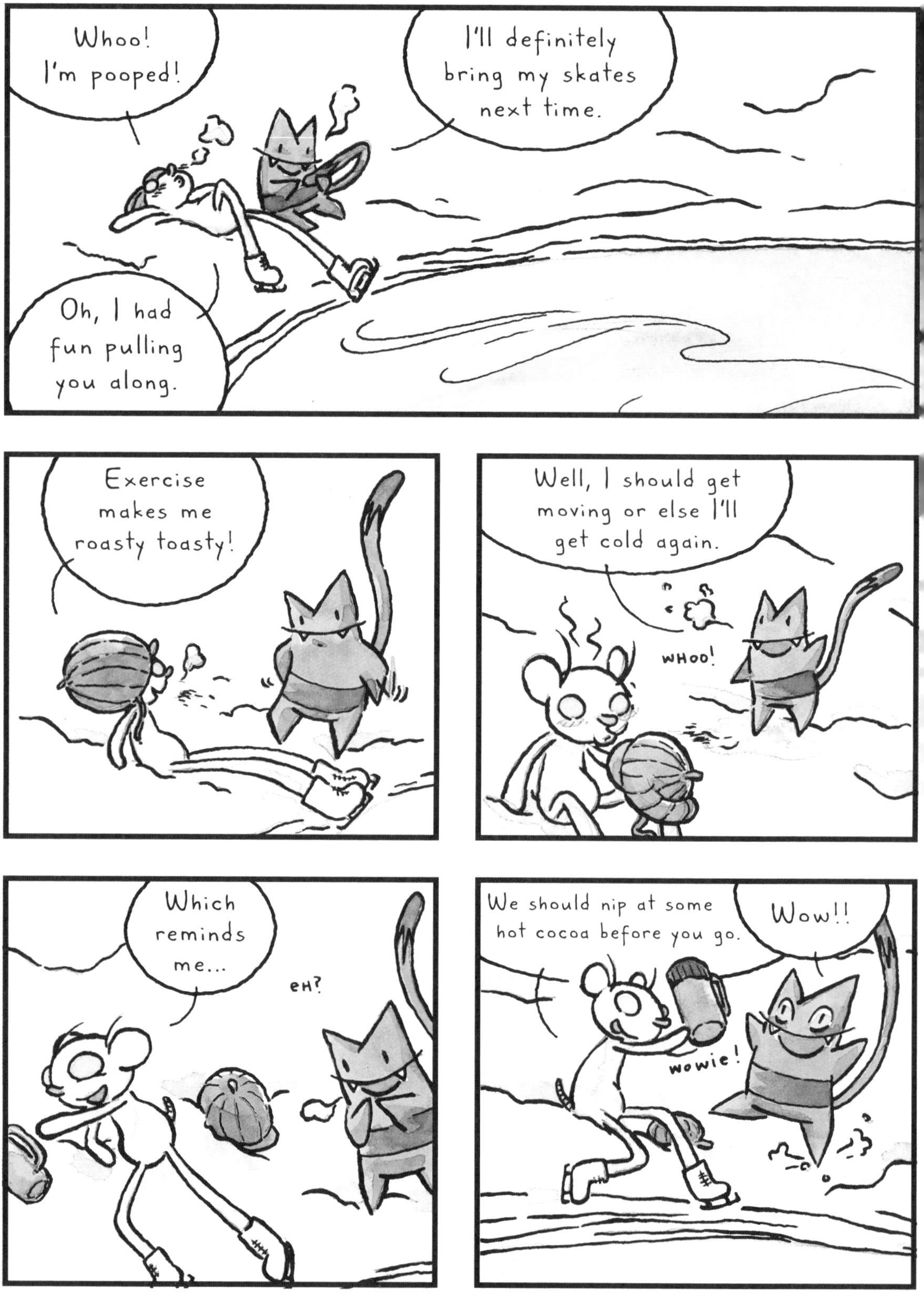
Whoo! I'm pooped!
I'll definitely bring my skates next time.
Oh, I had fun pulling you along.
Exercise makes me roasty toasty!
Well, I should get moving or else I'll get cold again.
WHOO!
Which reminds me...
EH?
We should nip at some hot cocoa before you go.
Wow!!
wowie!

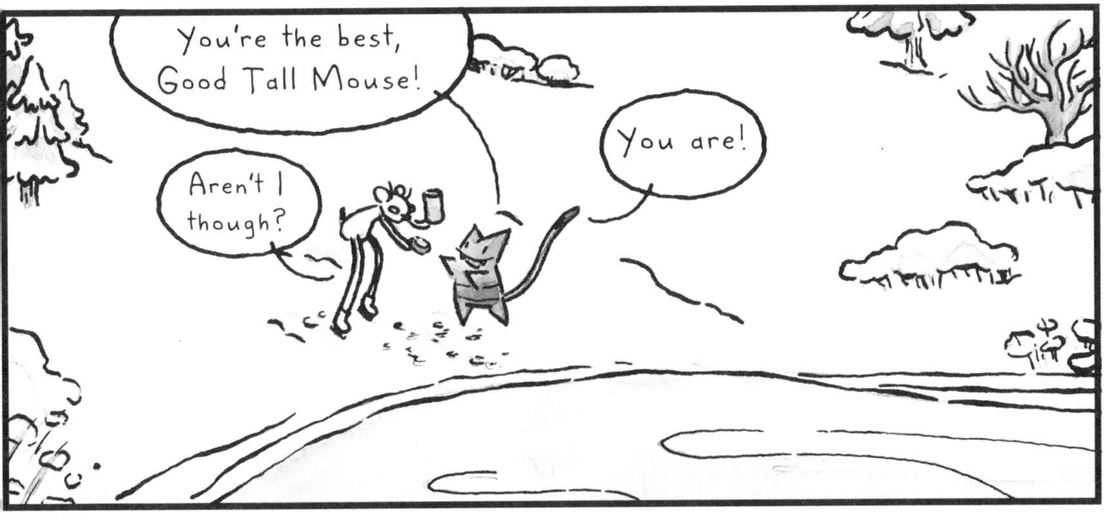
You're the best, Good Tall Mouse!
Aren't I though?
You are!

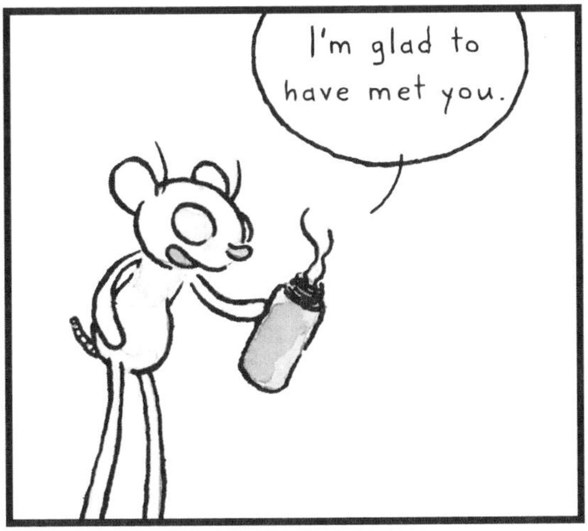
I'm glad to have met you.

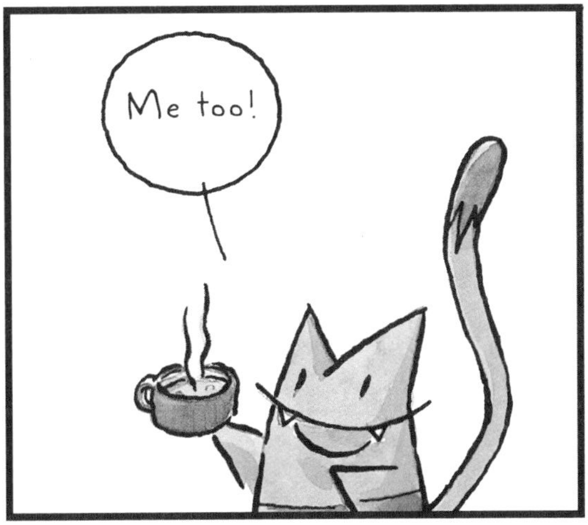
Me too!

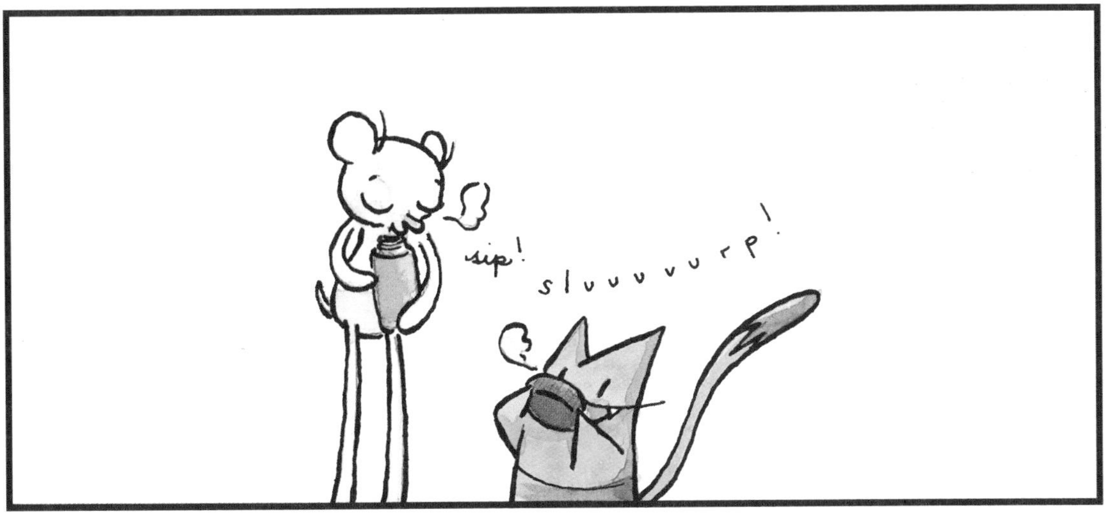
sip!
sluuuuurp!

Food Fests
Are the Best

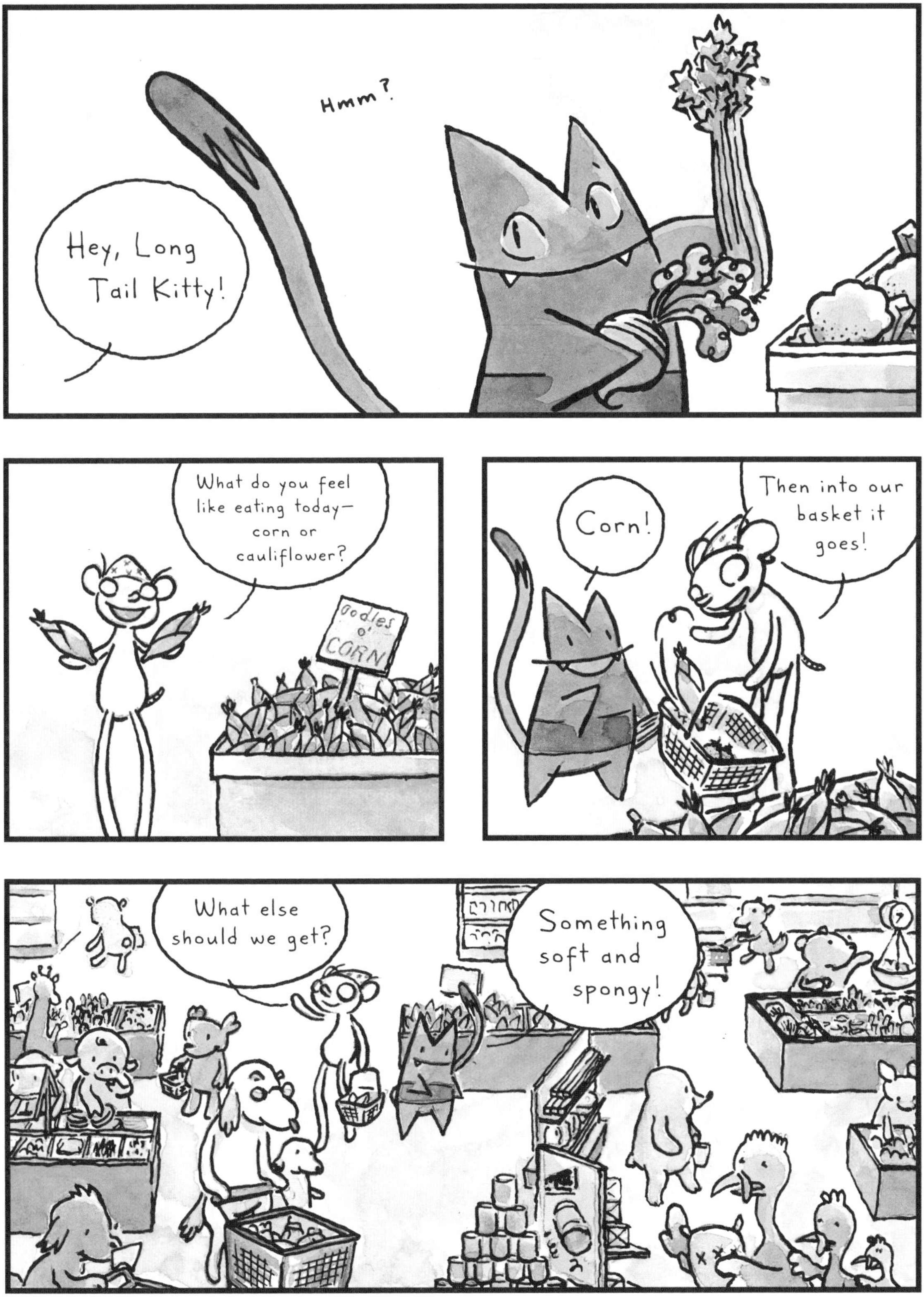
Hey, Long Tail Kitty!
Hmm?
What do you feel like eating today— corn or cauliflower?
Oodles o' CORN
Corn!
Then into our basket it goes!
What else should we get?
Something soft and spongy!

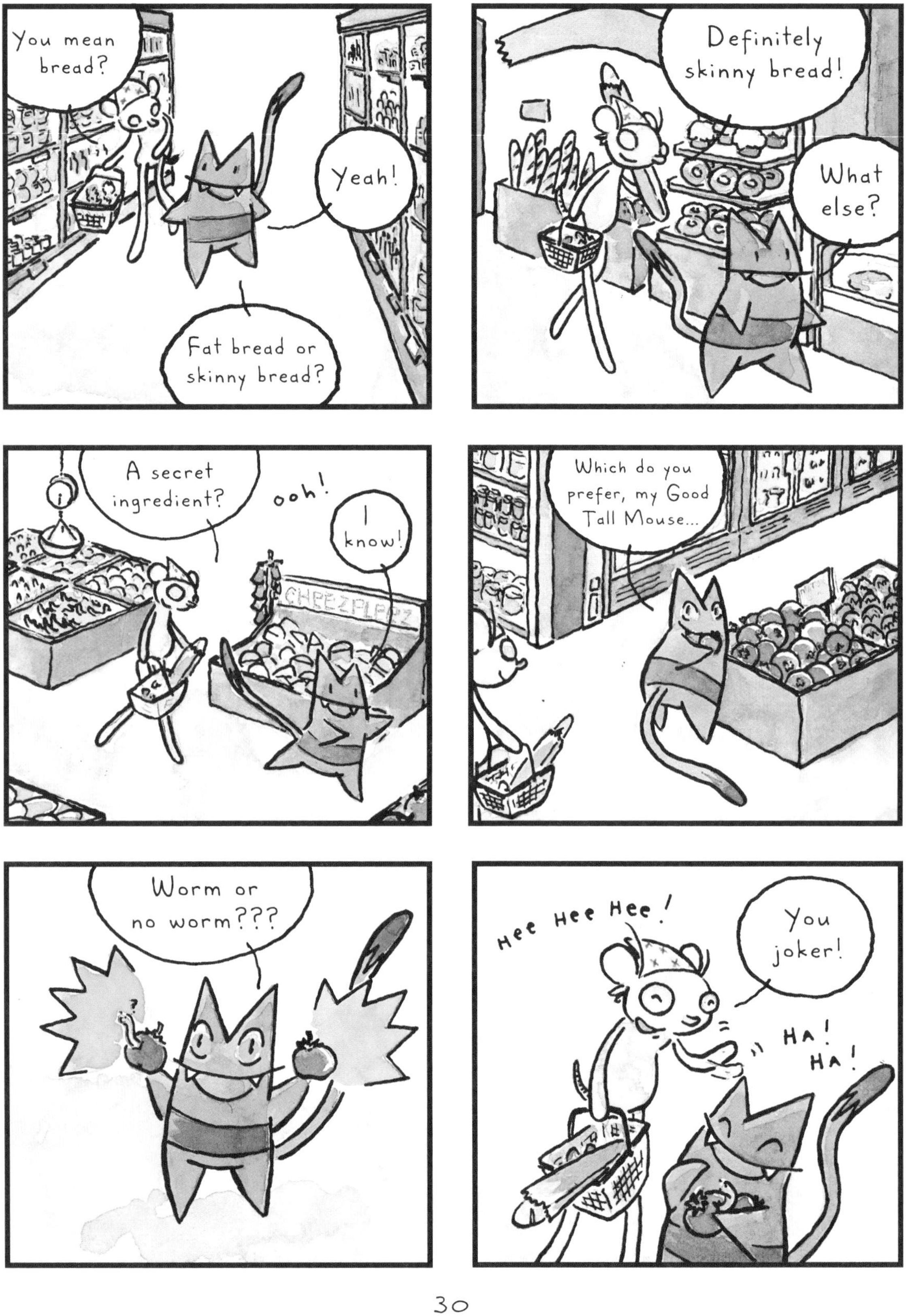
You mean bread?
Yeah!
Fat bread or skinny bread?
Definitely skinny bread!
What else?
A secret ingredient?
ooh!
I know!
CHEEZPLPPZ
Which do you prefer, my Good Tall Mouse...
Worm or no worm???
Hee Hee Hee!
You joker!
HA! HA!

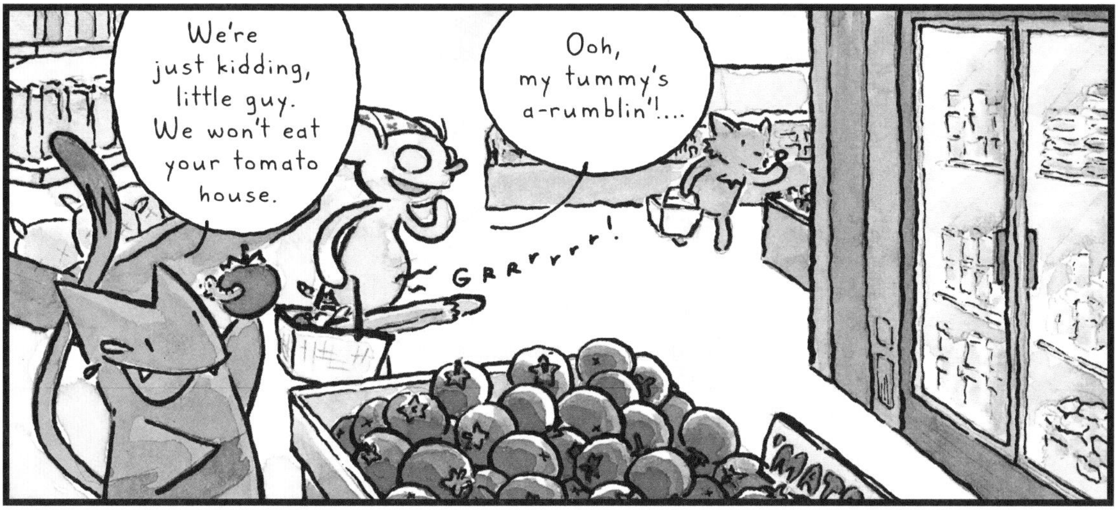
We're just kidding, little guy. We won't eat your tomato house.
Ooh, my tummy's a-rumblin'!...
GRRrrrr!

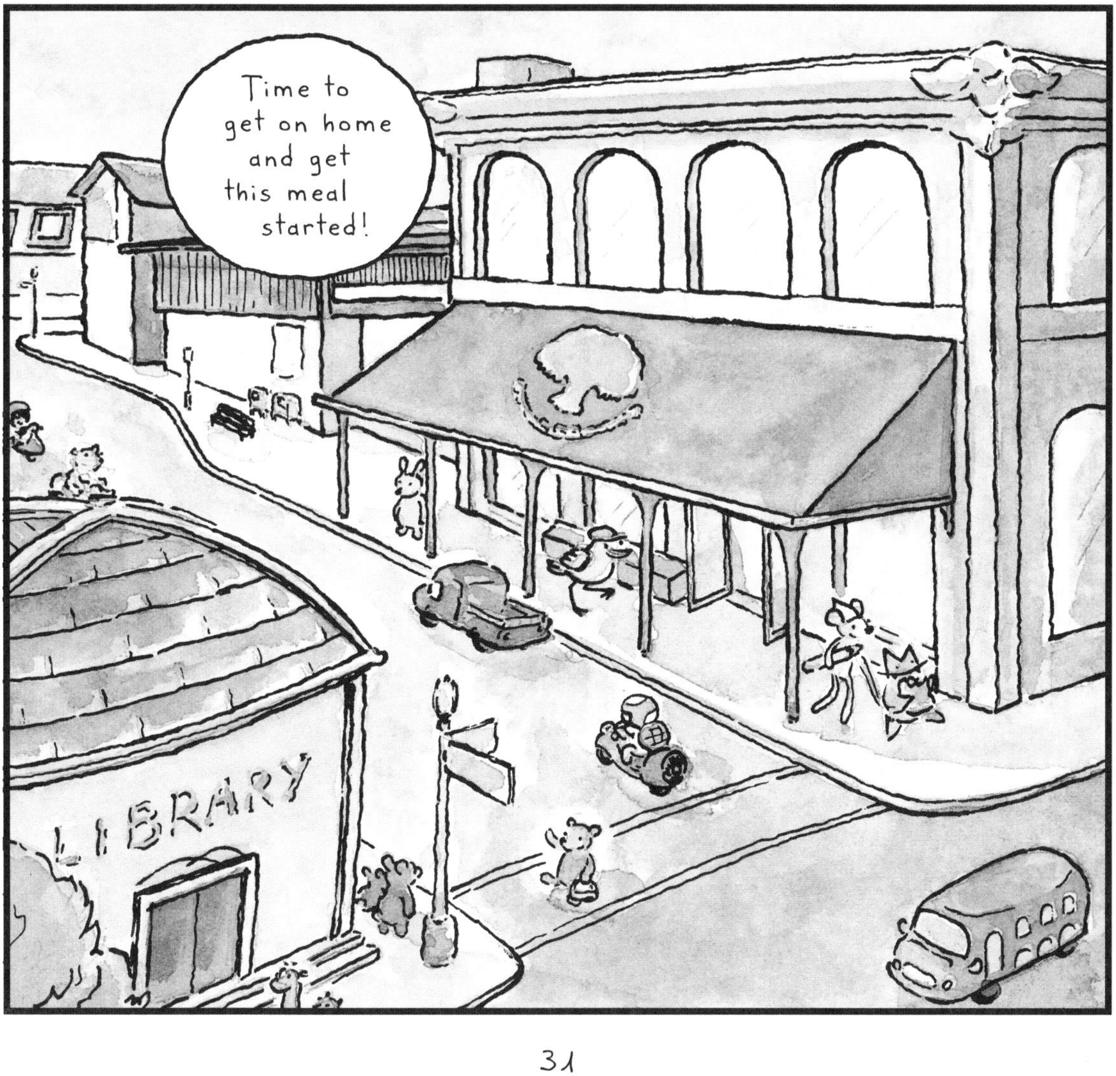
Time to get on home and get this meal started!
LIBRARY

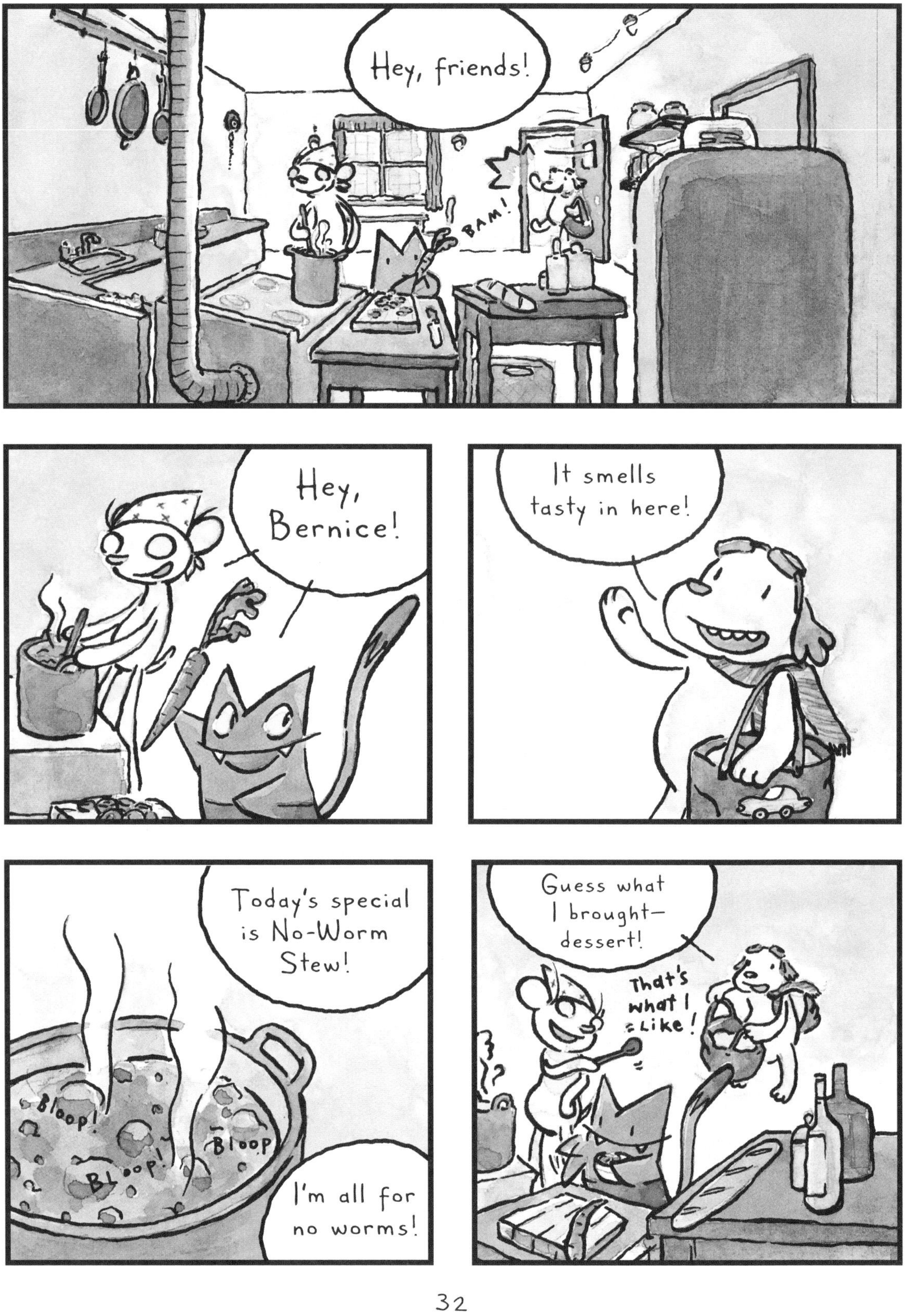
Hey, friends!
BAM!
Hey, Bernice!
It smells tasty in here!
Today's special is No-Worm Stew!
Bloop!
Bloop!
Bloop
I'm all for no worms!
Guess what I brought—dessert!
That's what I like!

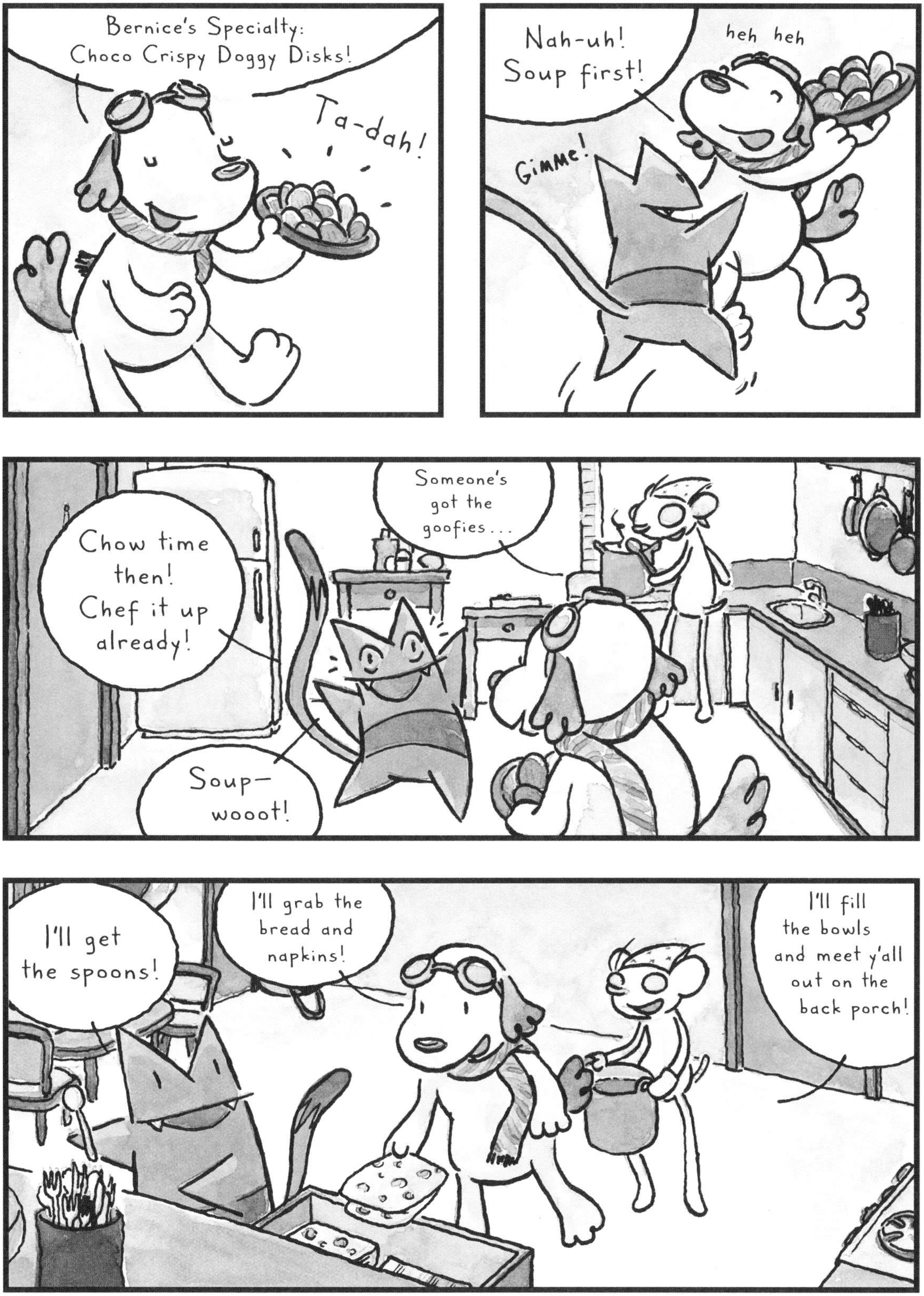
Bernice's Specialty: Choco Crispy Doggy Disks!
Ta-dah!
Nah-uh! Soup first!
heh heh
Gimme!
Chow time then! Chef it up already!
Someone's got the goofies...
Soup—wooot!
I'll get the spoons!
I'll grab the bread and napkins!
I'll fill the bowls and meet y'all out on the back porch!

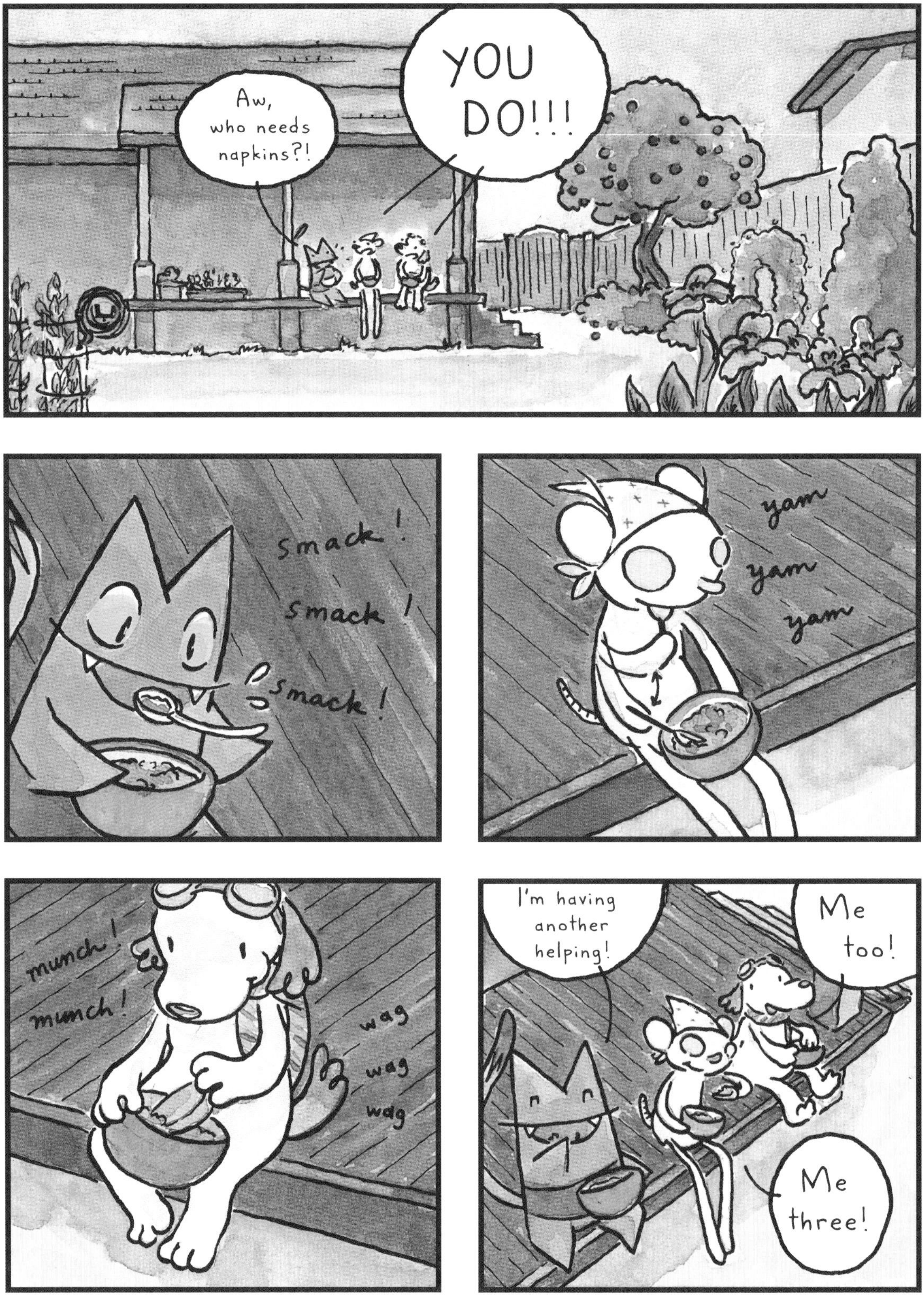
Aw, who needs napkins?!
YOU DO!!!
smack!
smack!
smack!
yam
yam
yam
munch!
munch!
wag
wag
wag
I'm having another helping!
Me too!
Me three!

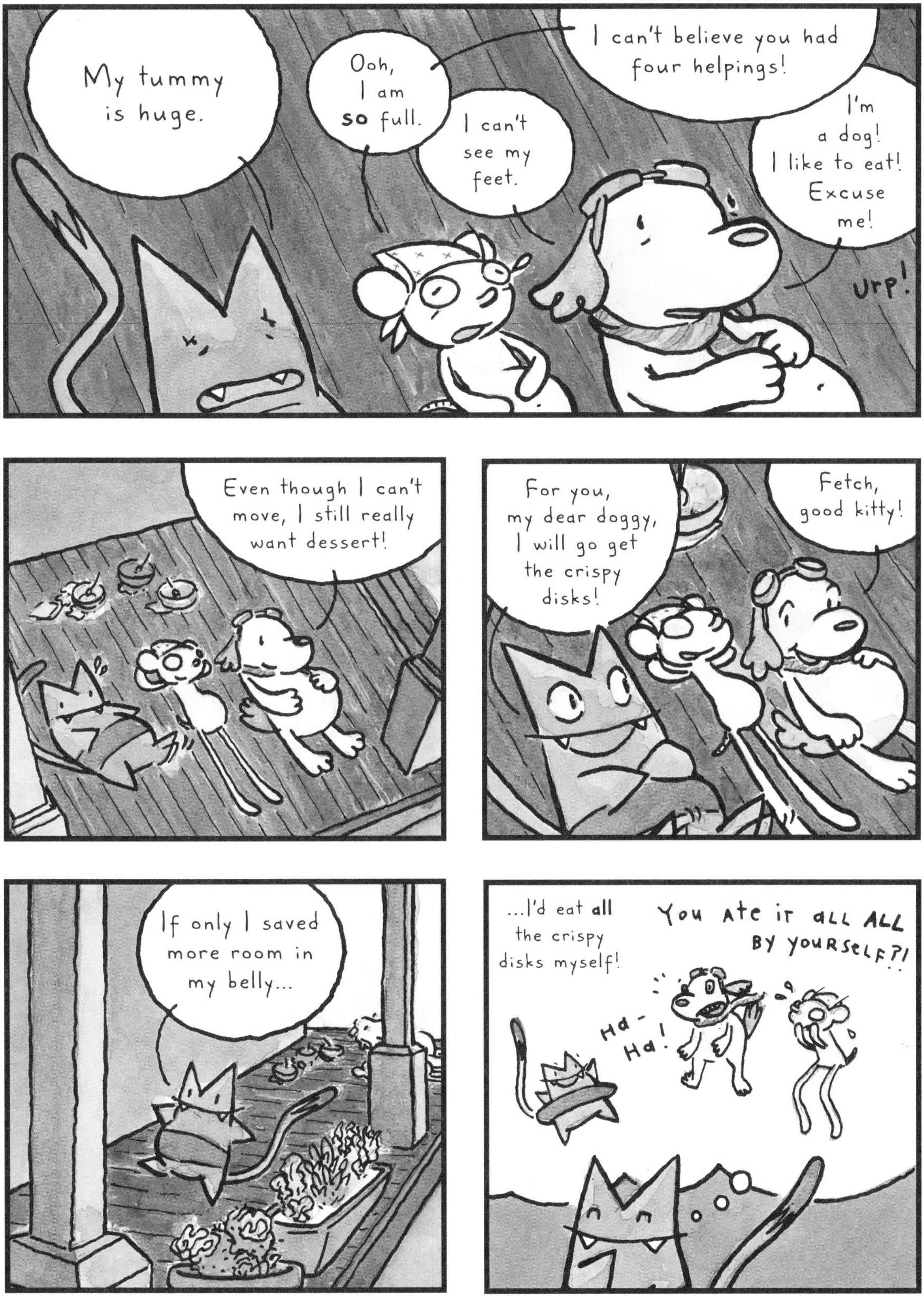
My tummy is huge.
Ooh, I am **so** full.
I can't believe you had four helpings!
I can't see my feet.
I'm a dog! I like to eat! Excuse me!
Urp!
Even though I can't move, I still really want dessert!
For you, my dear doggy, I will go get the crispy disks!
Fetch, good kitty!
If only I saved more room in my belly...
...I'd eat **all** the crispy disks myself!
You ate it all ALL by yourself?!
Ha-Ha!

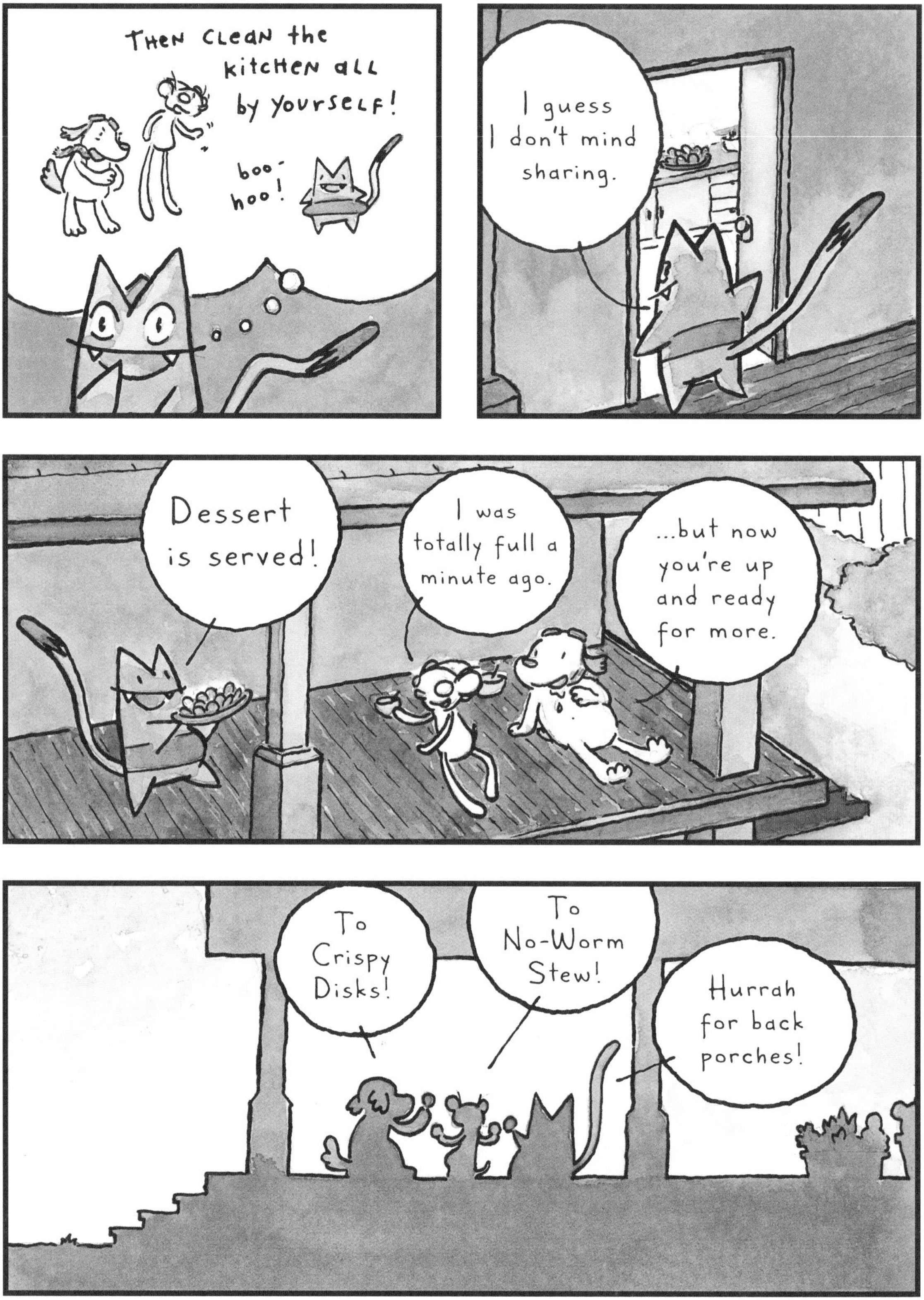
THEN CLEAN the KITCHEN ALL by YOURSELF!
boo-hoo!
I guess I don't mind sharing.
Dessert is served!
I was totally full a minute ago.
...but now you're up and ready for more.
To Crispy Disks!
To No-Worm Stew!
Hurrah for back porches!

Though We're Far,
We're Friends

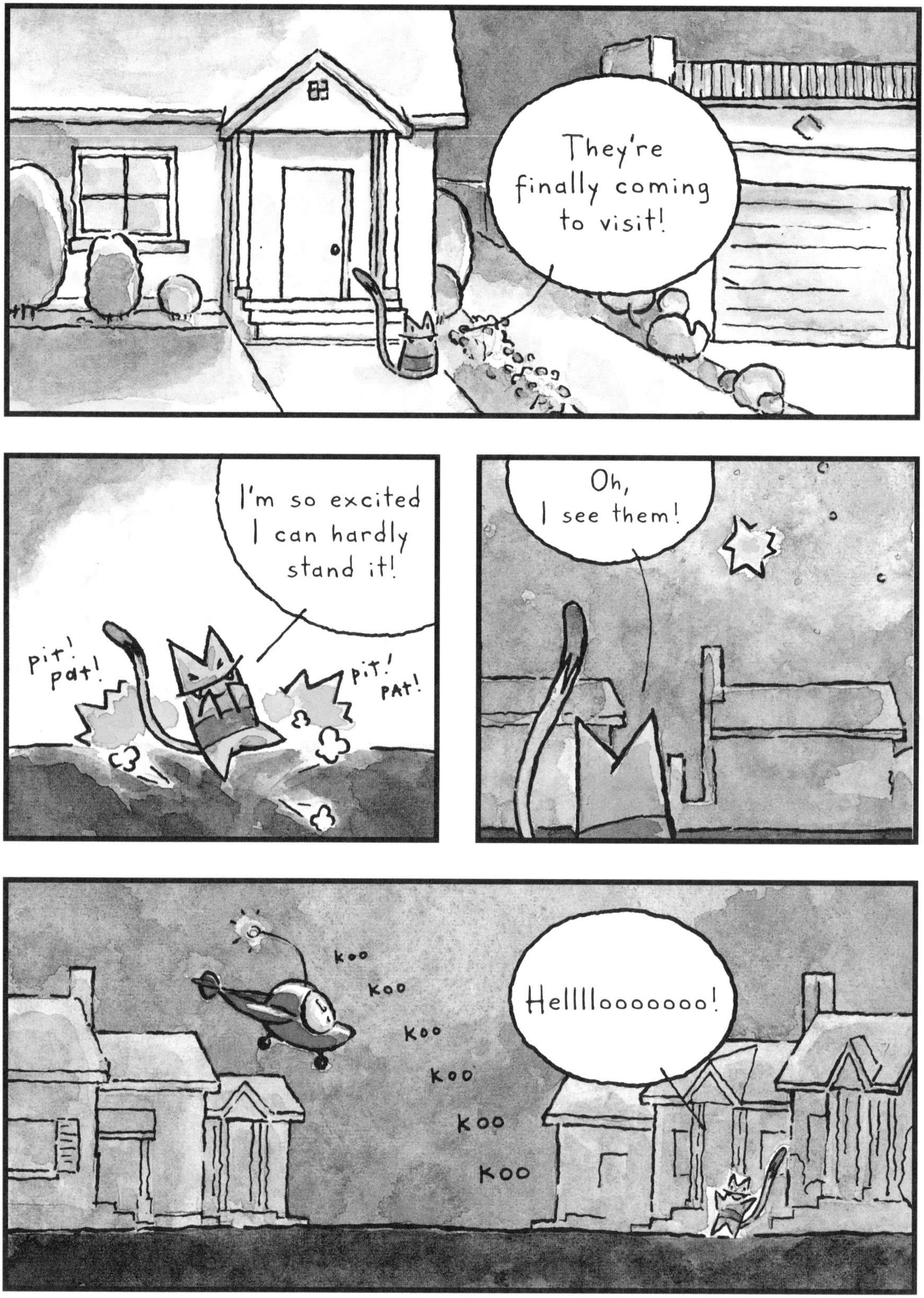
They're finally coming to visit!
I'm so excited I can hardly stand it!
pit! pat!
pit! pat!
Oh, I see them!
koo
koo
koo
koo
koo
koo
Hellllooooooo!

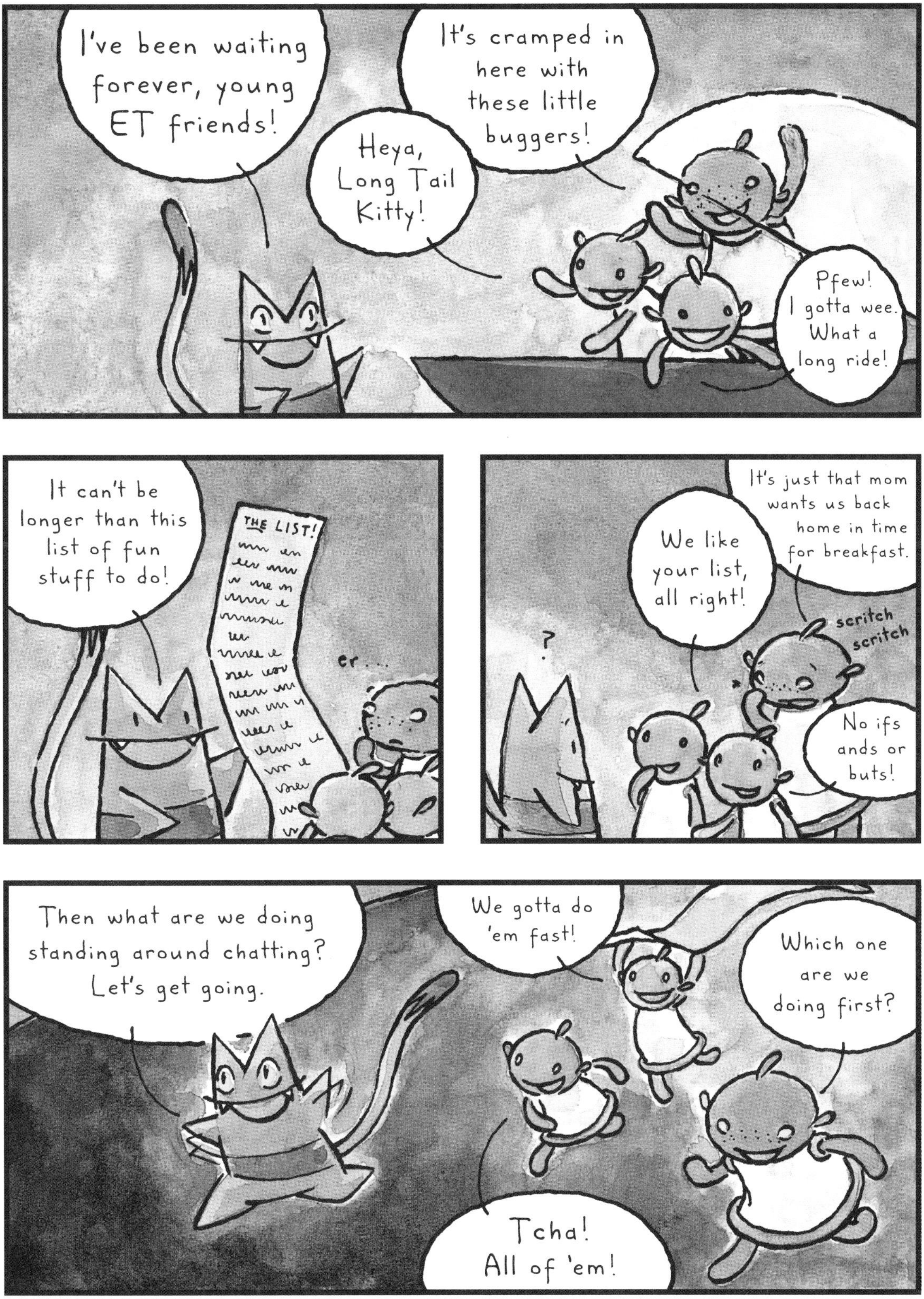
I've been waiting forever, young ET friends!
It's cramped in here with these little buggers!
Heya, Long Tail Kitty!
Pfew! I gotta wee. What a long ride!
It can't be longer than this list of fun stuff to do!
THE LIST!
er...
It's just that mom wants us back home in time for breakfast.
We like your list, all right!
?
scritch scritch
No ifs ands or buts!
Then what are we doing standing around chatting? Let's get going.
We gotta do 'em fast!
Which one are we doing first?
Tcha! All of 'em!

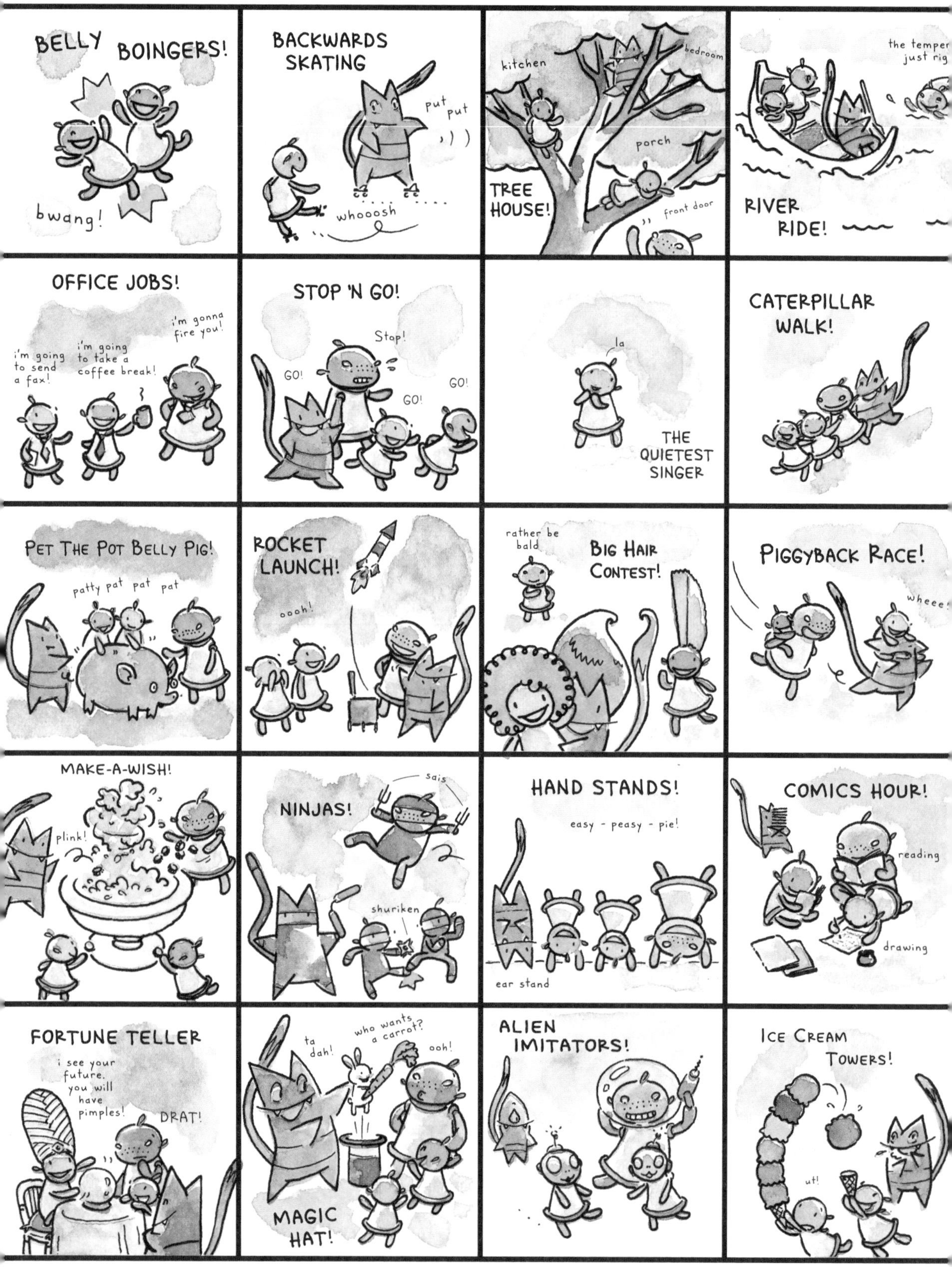
BELLY BOINGERS!
bwang!
BACKWARDS SKATING
put put
whooosh
kitchen
bedroom
porch
front door
TREE HOUSE!
RIVER RIDE!
OFFICE JOBS!
i'm going to send a fax!
i'm going to take a coffee break!
i'm gonna fire you!
STOP 'N GO!
Stop!
GO!
GO!
GO!
la
THE QUIETEST SINGER
CATERPILLAR WALK!
PET THE POT BELLY PIG!
patty pat pat pat
ROCKET LAUNCH!
oooh!
rather be bald
BIG HAIR CONTEST!
PIGGYBACK RACE!
MAKE-A-WISH!
plink!
NINJAS!
sais
shuriken
HAND STANDS!
easy - peasy - pie!
ear stand
COMICS HOUR!
reading
drawing
FORTUNE TELLER
i see your future. you will have pimples!
DRAT!
ta dah!
who wants a carrot?
ooh!
MAGIC HAT!
ALIEN IMITATORS!
ICE CREAM TOWERS!
uh!

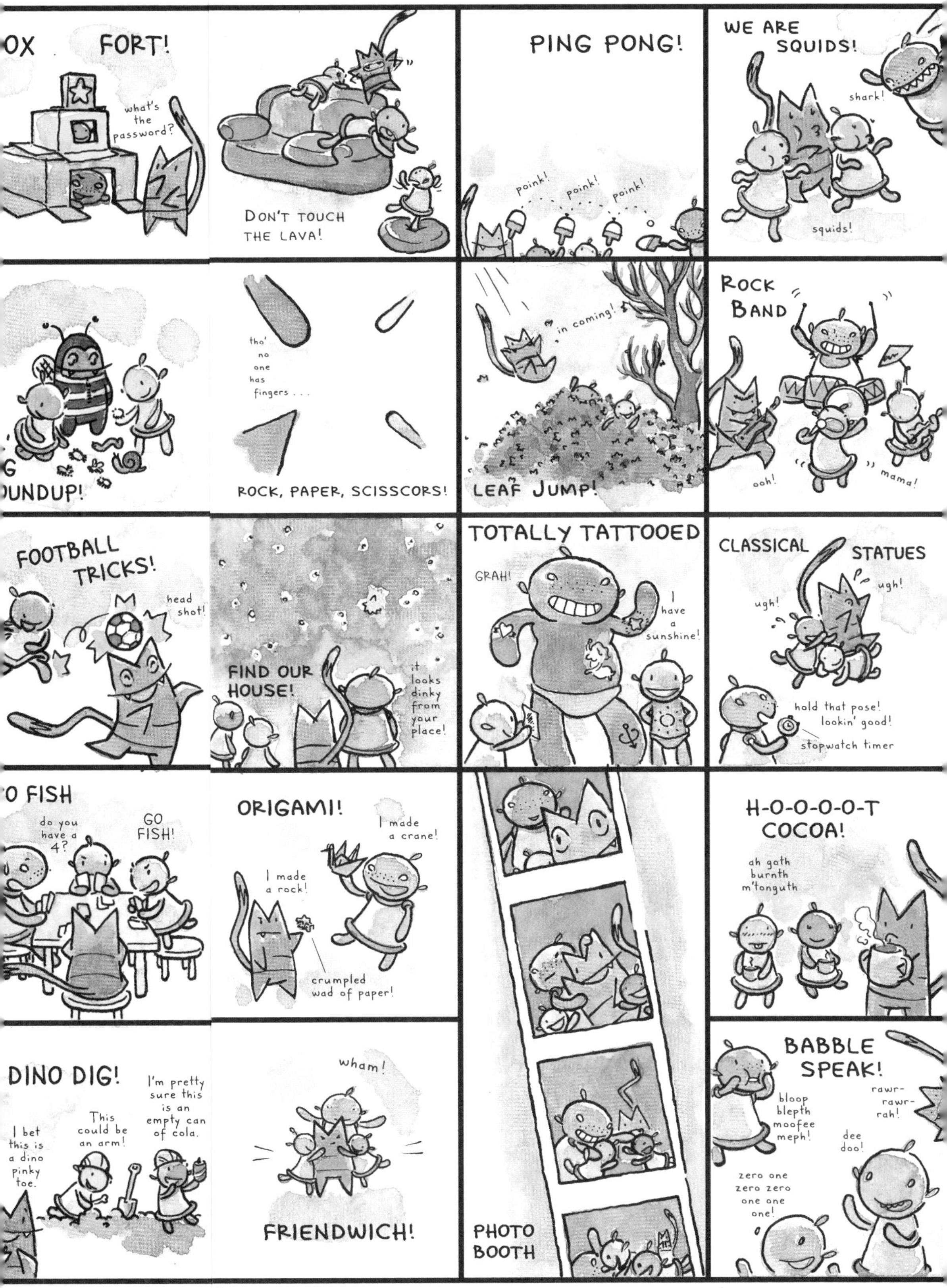

OX FORT!
what's the password?
DON'T TOUCH THE LAVA!
PING PONG!
poink!
poink!
poink!
WE ARE SQUIDS!
shark!
squids!
G
UNDUP!
tho' no one has fingers . . .
ROCK, PAPER, SCISSCORS!
in coming!
LEAF JUMP!
ROCK BAND
ooh!
mama!
FOOTBALL TRICKS!
head shot!
FIND OUR HOUSE!
it looks dinky from your place!
TOTALLY TATTOOED
GRAH!
I have a sunshine!
CLASSICAL STATUES
ugh!
ugh!
hold that pose! lookin' good!
stopwatch timer
O FISH
do you have a 4?
GO FISH!
ORIGAMI!
I made a crane!
I made a rock!
crumpled wad of paper!
H-O-O-O-O-T COCOA!
ah goth burnth m'tonguth
DINO DIG!
I bet this is a dino pinky toe.
This could be an arm!
I'm pretty sure this is an empty can of cola.
wham!
FRIENDWICH!
PHOTO BOOTH
BABBLE SPEAK!
bloop blepth moofee meph!
rawr-rawr-rah!
dee doo!
zero one zero zero one one one!

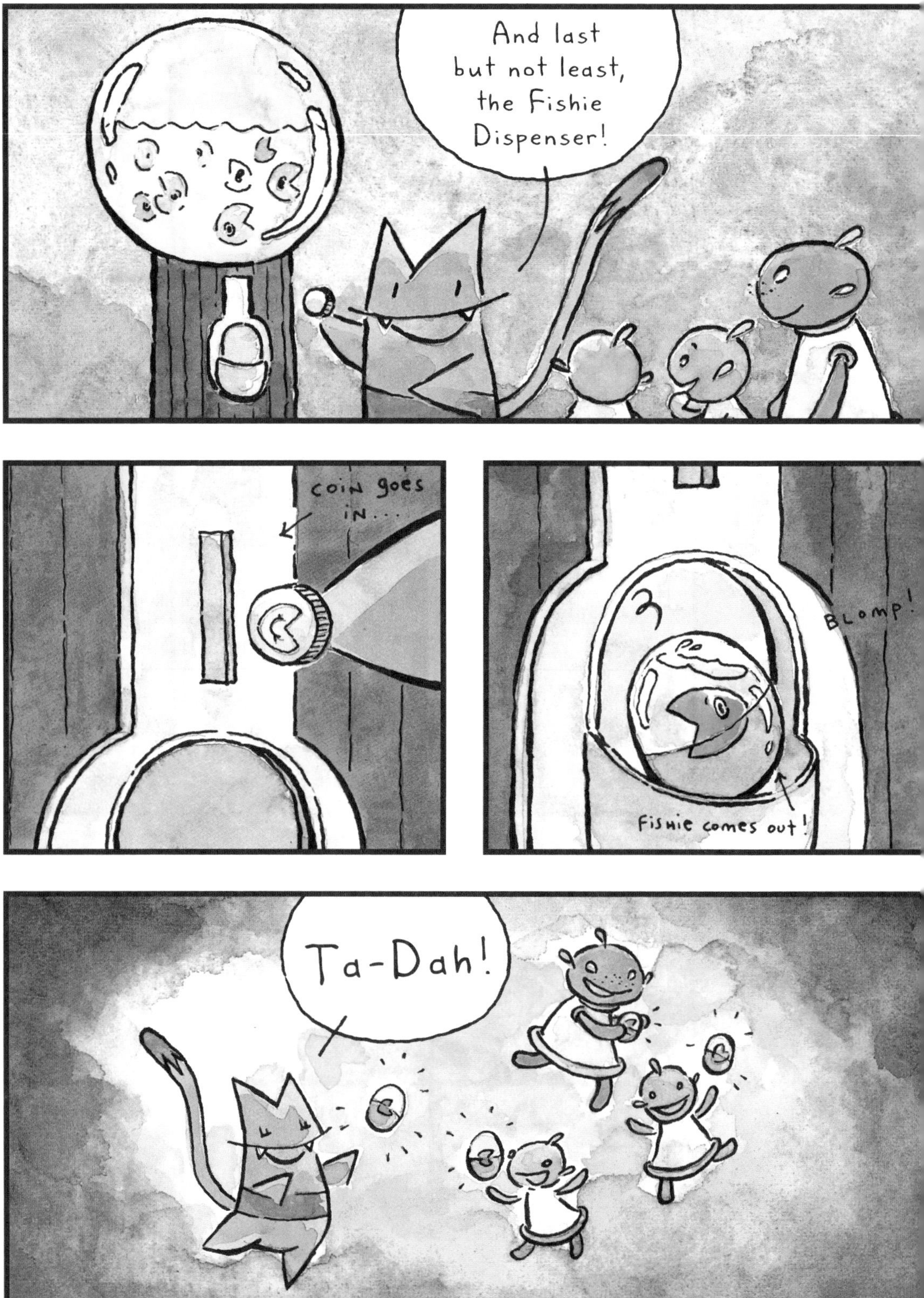
And last but not least, the Fishie Dispenser!
COIN goes IN...
BLOMP!
FISHIE comes out!
Ta-Dah!

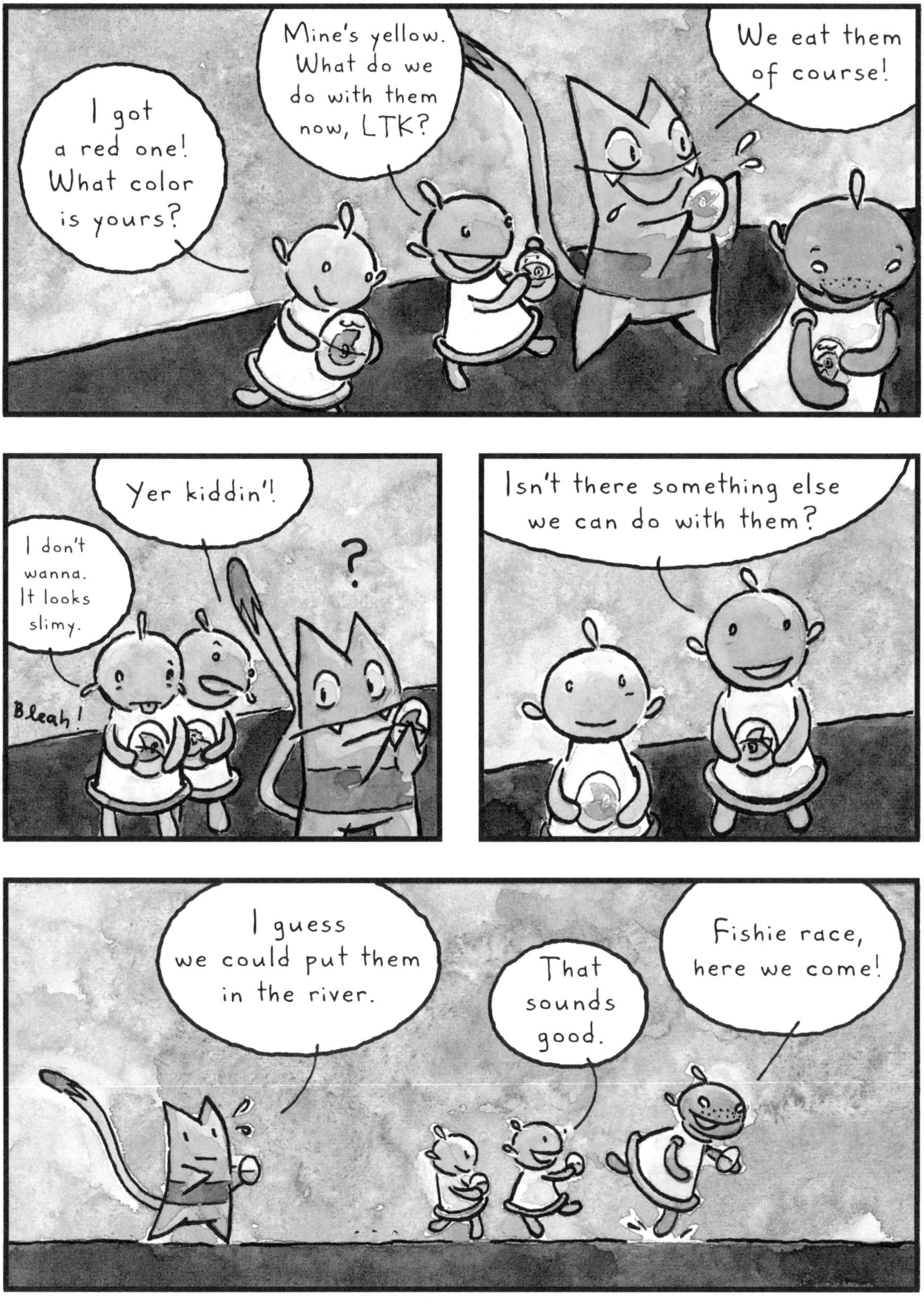
I got a red one! What color is yours?
Mine's yellow. What do we do with them now, LTK?
We eat them of course!
Yer kiddin'!
I don't wanna. It looks slimy.
Bleah!
?
Isn't there something else we can do with them?
I guess we could put them in the river.
That sounds good.
Fishie race, here we come!

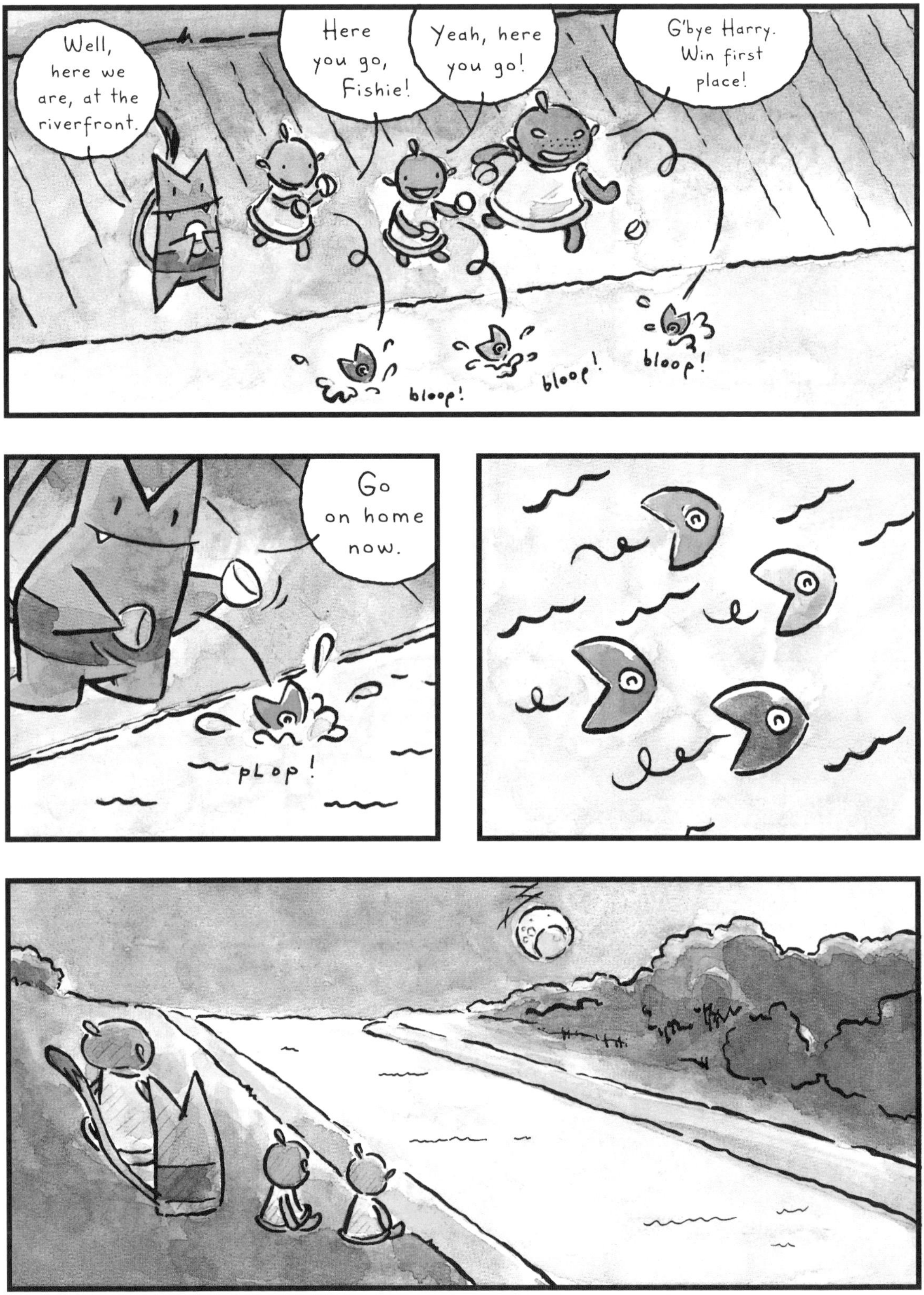
Well, here we are, at the riverfront.
Here you go, Fishie!
Yeah, here you go!
G'bye Harry. Win first place!
bloop!
bloop!
bloop!
Go on home now.
pLop!

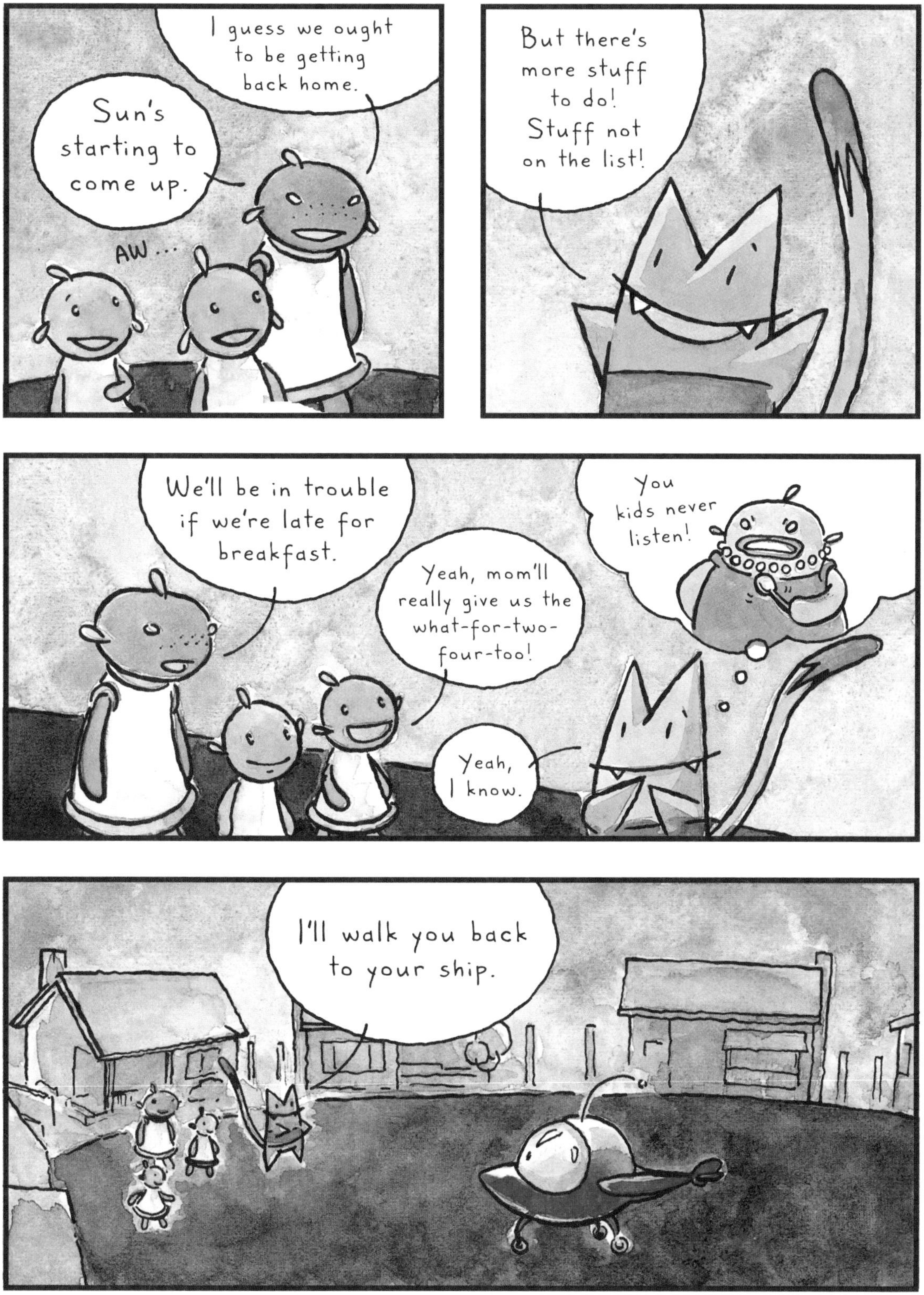
I guess we ought to be getting back home.
Sun's starting to come up.
AW...
But there's more stuff to do! Stuff not on the list!
We'll be in trouble if we're late for breakfast.
Yeah, mom'll really give us the what-for-two-four-too!
You kids never listen!
Yeah, I know.
I'll walk you back to your ship.

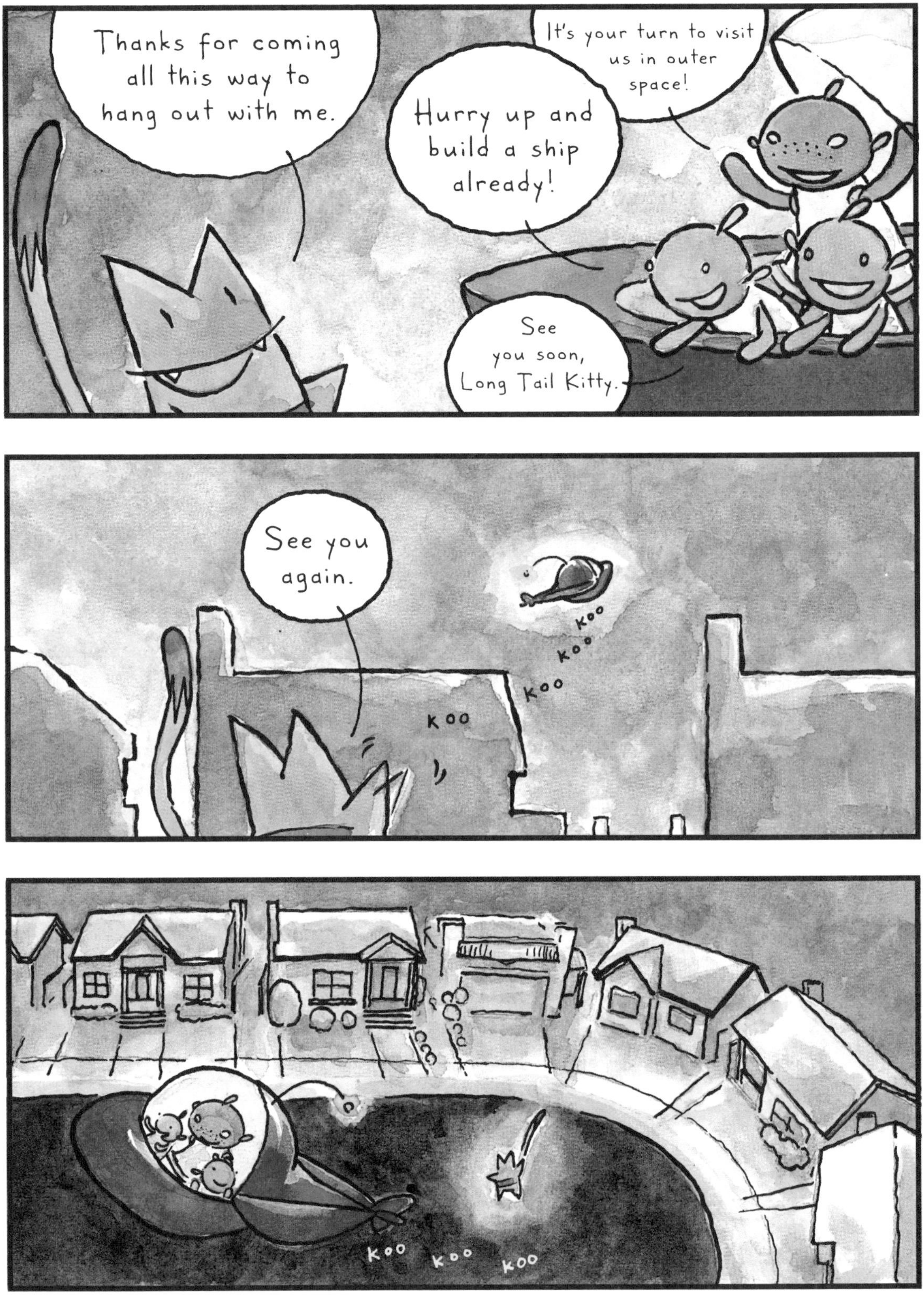
Thanks for coming all this way to hang out with me.
It's your turn to visit us in outer space!
Hurry up and build a ship already!
See you soon, Long Tail Kitty.
See you again.
KOO
KOO
KOO
KOO
KOO KOO KOO

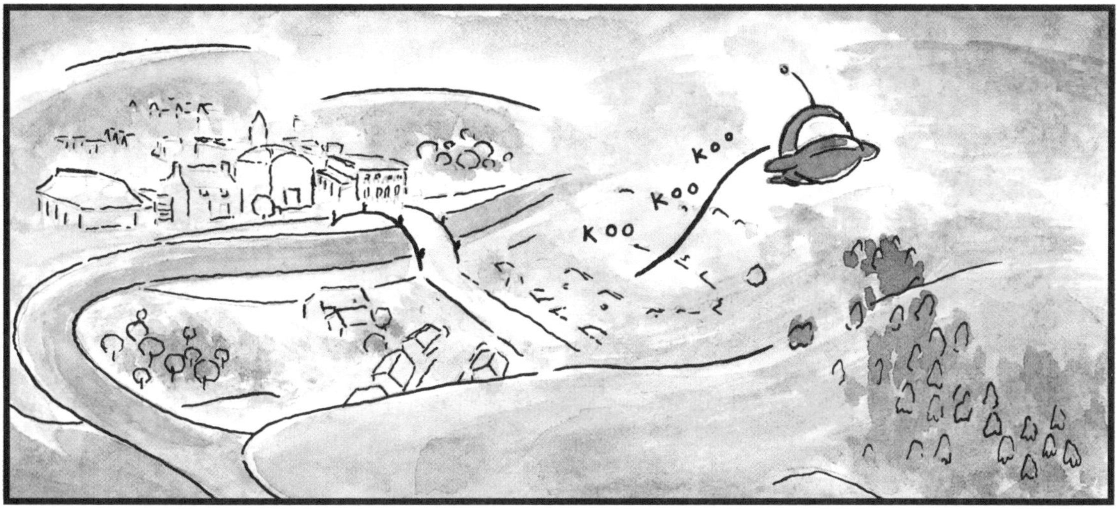
KOO
KOO
KOO

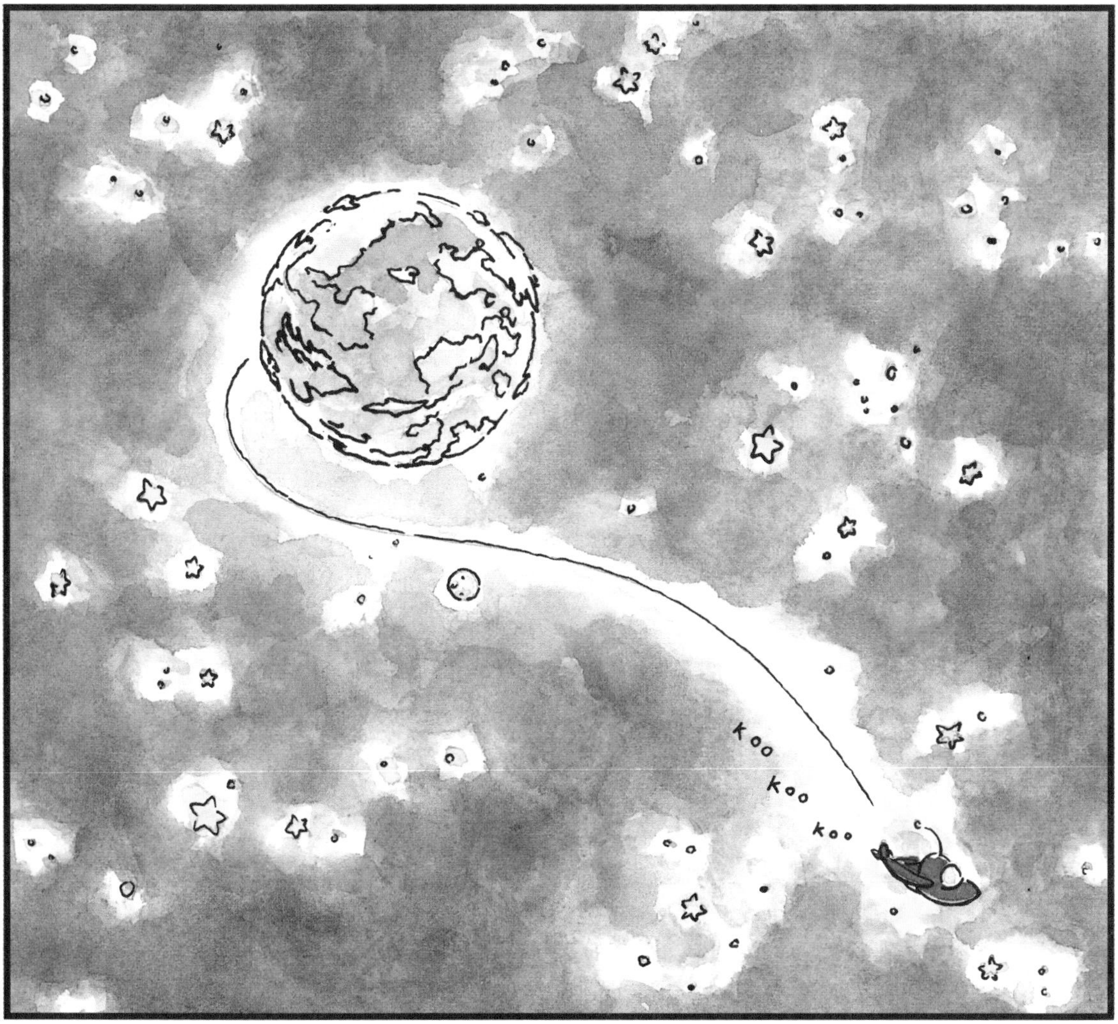
KOO
KOO
KOO

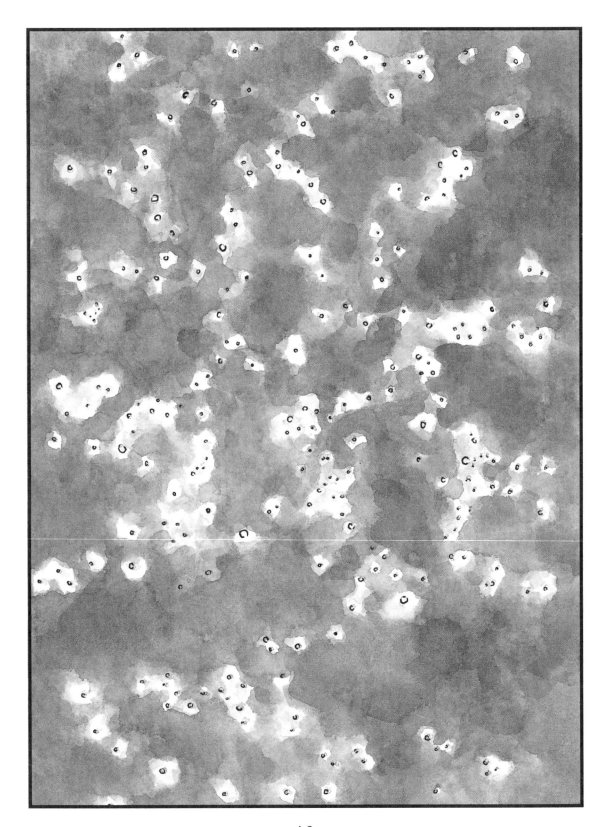

48

BONUS PAGES

How To Draw Long Tail Kitty

Looks like
The Letter "M"

1. START WITH HIS EARS

His legs
are a little
further
apart than
his ears

2. ADD HIS LEGS AND TUMMY

Tuck his
eyes under
the ears

Draw his
mouth + whiskers
using one line!

Add a
curve and
his
mouth
is
open!

Little
triangles for
teeth

3. DRAW HIS EYES AND MOUTH

His arms
are
pointy!

His stripe is a
big and thick
bellywarmer!

Point them
in all kinds of
directions!

4. ADD HIS ARMS AND STRIPE

Very, very
important!:
Don't forget to
draw his tail!

...or else he
will be
No Tail Kitty.

5. AND LAST HIS TAIL-
MAKE IT LONG!

Tah-Dah!

NOW CELEBRATE!

The Many Moods of Long Tail Kitty

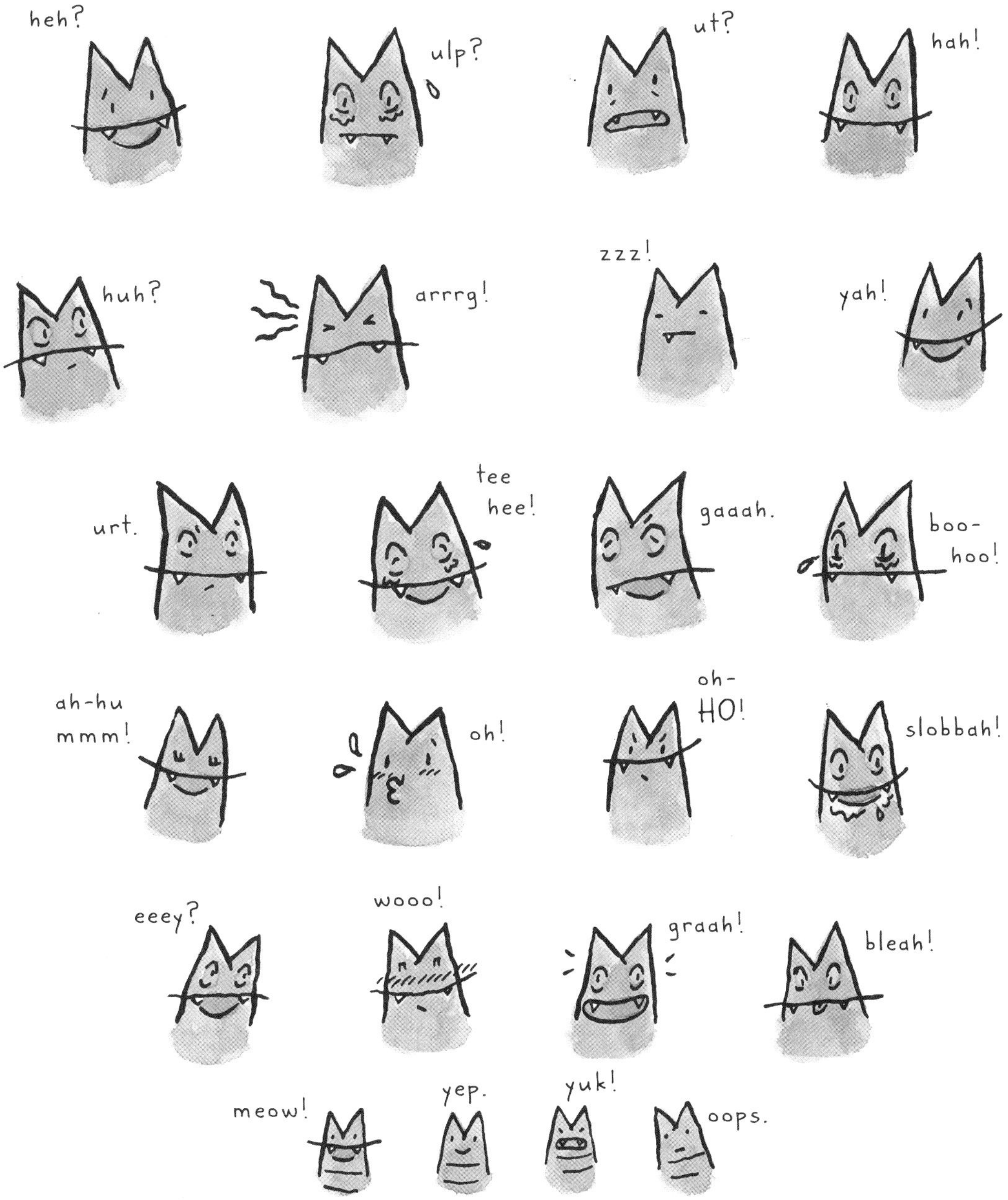
heh?
ulp?
ut?
hah!
huh?
arrrg!
zzz!
yah!
urt.
tee hee!
gaaah.
boo-hoo!
ah-hu mmm!
oh!
oh-HO!
slobbah!
eeey?
wooo!
graah!
bleah!
meow!
yep.
yuk!
oops.

What sort of faces do you make? Draw some of your own!